BURN ME OUT

BRANDON BARROWS

Black Rose Writing | Texas

ISBN: 978-1-68433-543-5
PUBLISHED BY BLACK ROSE WRITING
www.blackrosewriting.com

Printed in the United States of America
Suggested Retail Price (SRP) $16.95

Burn Me Out is printed in Book Antiqua

*As a planet-friendly publisher, Black Rose Writing does its best to eliminate unnecessary waste to reduce paper usage and energy costs, while never compromising the reading experience. As a result, the final word count vs. page count may not meet common expectations.

For everyone with their back against the wall.

BURN ME OUT

"There's a right way to live and a right way to die... but who the hell knows what it is?"
- Chiaki Kuriyama, *Cold Finger Girl*

1

The lead pipe slammed into Sal Brentano's head with a sickening thump and down he went, collapsing like a bloodied, string-cut marionette onto the pavement.

The sound of the falling body — *fwump* – echoed, for just an instant, in the narrow, trash-strewn alleyway. His legs twitched, first one, then the other, and then he was still.

"Ha! Ya see that, Al?" Benny crowed, eyes wide with joy and violence, his gaze flicking back and forth between the stained length of metal in his hand and the crumpled, bloodied figure at his feet. A faint moaning sound worked its way from the dying man's throat and a shudder ran through his body. Brentano hadn't cowered, hadn't whimpered, before the blow was struck - he simply stood there and took it like he knew this was inevitable. But now, as his life literally drained from him, instinct took over and he fought—however meaninglessly — against the end.

From the mouth of the alley, Al, the elder of the pair, answered, "I saw," though he couldn't have; his back was to the alley, facing out toward the street, scanning for potential interruptions or unwanted observers. In this part of town, at this time of night, it was unlikely, but why take chances?

Audience or no, Benny watched his own handiwork, fascinated, as the man before him struggled, unconscious for all purposes — his head leaking blood and something that resembled clam chowder mixed with raspberry jam — until the faint, weak movements slowed, ebbed and finally stopped. Benny grinned. Death was a miracle, and he didn't want to miss an instant of it.

Less than five minutes had passed, by Al's estimation, since the pair and their "guest" had entered the alley behind the small warehouse belonging to Brentano's Imports. It was almost time to go. Al had to give Brentano credit where it was due, though: he was at least making this easy on them. After the initial offer of bribes (with money he didn't have) or bargains (without anything, really, to offer), the man had hardly been any trouble at all. No escape attempts, no trying for any hidden gun or blade in the small office where Al and Benny had confronted him. Brentano knew what he'd done, knew why they were there and, after only token verbal resistance, he seemed to accept that this was simply inevitable – the results of his own actions. Al appreciated that.

But did Benny? Al wondered.

Safely out of earshot of Brentano's nightshift crew, Benny had wasted no time in getting down to the business at hand, but now he was dragging his feet, taking his time, enjoying his own handiwork. Enough was enough. No need to keep indulging the kid's sickness.

"Benny, you 'bout done there?"

Slowly, as if waking from a pleasant dream, Benny turned towards the other man, his grin turning even wider. "You see, Al? One hit, down he goes. Didn't even have to give him another whack."

Al snorted and made a pretense of checking his watch, all but impossible in this dimness, so far from the nearest streetlight. It wasn't enough the kid got his rocks off on this kind of shit, he needed to be praised for it, too? A hint of queasiness spread through Al's belly.

"Don't get such a big head, kid. He's just some old feeb."

"Yeah." Benny's grin turned feral as his lip curled upward into a sort of snarl. Combined with his sharp, slightly crooked nose, it made him look like some huge, pale bird of prey. "Yeah," he said again, more slowly, then spat on the broken thing that had moments ago been a man named Salvatore Brentano, adding insult to mortal injury. He tossed the pipe down, hard, for good measure. It made a hollow *thump* sound before rolling off the man's back to clatter onto the ground. "Just a deadbeat, piece'a shit feeb."

Al suppressed a sigh and turned away. "Let's go, before someone sees us." He headed up the street, not waiting to see if Benny would follow or not, expensive Italian leather shoe-soles slapping softly against cracked pavement. If it was up to him, he'd have left alone, but very little was left to him these days. For the moment, there was nothing to do but go along with it.

Benny took a last look at his night's work before turning and following, jogging a few steps to catch up. He was a little crazy, but he wasn't stupid; Al was his ride, after all.

Falling in line beside the man who was supposed to be his mentor, Benny said, "You worry too much in your old age, Al."

Al sneered out of the side of his mouth, glad the car was only around the corner. He dug in his pocket for the keys in preparation. For all his apparent calmness, though, it was true: Al was worried and he wanted to be gone from this spot as quickly as possible. The older he got, the less he liked this part of the job. It wasn't the death; he'd been dealing with that long enough. It wasn't Brentano himself; the man had made choices he clearly knew, and apparently accepted, the consequences of. The stupid sort of double-cross he'd pulled made no sense, but the why didn't bother Al, either. He hadn't even known the guy. His death meant nothing to Al. It was simply another errand to run.

No, none of that was the problem.

It was that Al had been lucky – not once, not twice, but over and over again for decades. And with each subsequent roll of the dice, the probability that his luck would run out grew higher.

3

But he couldn't admit that, not to Benny at least, so all he said was: "I'm only forty-six."

Benny cackled.

***

Al pulled his gray, older model Crown Victoria into the off-street parking area of La Cucina Italiana and slid into a spot near the side of the building marked "STAFF." He wasn't, but nobody would complain. Benny was out of the passenger-side door—slamming it too hard behind him—and heading around the front of the restaurant before Al had even taken the key out of the ignition. If there was one thing to be said for Benny, it was that he didn't lack for enthusiasm.

Taking a moment to check his mirror and make sure he looked presentable—this was a nice restaurant—Al followed at a more sedate pace. He was pleasantly surprised to see that Benny had waited on the sidewalk in front of the restaurant instead of simply rushing inside and was now using the building's large, plate-glass window to smooth his normally slicked-back hair—mussed from the evening's work—back into place. At least the kid recognized the need for decorum here.

Benny flashed a lazy half-smile at Al's reflection in the window. "What took ya?" The tone was friendly, easygoing, as if the two were simply there for a leisurely dinner. The act wouldn't fool anyone with eyes. Sure, the killer was hidden for now, but the evidence of his existence was in plain sight: Al winced at the speckles of blood spread across the cuffs of Benny's white suit-jacket.

The younger man finished arranging his hair and asked, "Well?"

Al shook it off and hoped Benny ordered something with marinara. "Nothing. Let's go." He pulled open the ornately framed glass door and gestured for Benny to precede him.

Inside, the pair entered a foyer decorated simply, but tastefully, with a wall-sized rack of vintage wine bottles to the left and, to the right, a table of fresh flowers beneath an arrangement of framed pastoral-themed prints. A waist-high chalkboard stood to one side of the table, showing the daily specials. The lighting emitted by the recessed ceiling fixtures was brighter than the evening outside, but only just, giving the small area a sense of coziness and intimacy.

A smiling, middle-aged maître d' in a black suit and tie, who was both somewhat smaller and somewhat older than Al, looked up from his little podium as the two men entered. To the man's credit, the smile remained in place even after he recognized them. "Mister Vacarro, good evening. Table for two, the usual place?"

Al grunted. It was a formality he didn't have the patience for tonight, but the guy was only doing his job. "Please."

"Right this way." The host headed into the interior of the restaurant, leaving his charges to follow.

Al knew the way well, and presumed Benny remembered, but appearances were important in this business; it wouldn't do for the two apparent customers to wander in unescorted at such a fine establishment. Chamber music whispered from hidden speakers overhead as they wove between tables of well-dressed diners and around wait-staff bearing heavily laden trays. Al allowed himself a tight, little smile, wondering if any of them knew who this place belonged to or what sort of dealings occurred right beneath their noses only a wall or two away. He glanced over his shoulder at Benny, whose head swiveled left and right, trying to take in the sights and sounds as they passed through this little slice of the upper-class. It was old-hat to Al, who had been in this place literally thousands of times over the years, but for Benny, still new to this world, the aging opulence of the restaurant must have seemed very impressive.

Al and Benny were led all the way through the main dining area, leaving behind the sounds of glasses clinking and silverware jangling against plates and bowls, past the private rooms that could be reserved by the general public for parties or meetings, through a door marked "STAFF ONLY" and finally, to the very back of the building where a last door, emblazoned with the word "PRIVATE," barred further progress.

The headwaiter raised a lightly balled fist to knock, but Al stopped him with a hand on his wrist. "I'll take it from here, Peter. Thank you."

Al released his grip. The man pulled his arm back, bowed his head slightly and took his leave without a word. Probably glad to go, Al guessed.

Al knocked. Once, twice – softly, just enough to be heard. The first time Benny had been here, before this door, almost three weeks ago now, he'd looked crestfallen and asked, "What, no secret code or nothin'?"

Almost instantly, the door swung open a crack and a sliver of face peered out, long enough to recognize the supplicants, before being thrown open all the way to reveal a tall, heavyset man in his early forties, clad in a rumpled brown suit. He nodded, stepped to the side and gestured, signaling that the pair could enter. He added, "Evening, Al."

Al nodded in return and squeezed past the larger man into the short hallway he guarded. "How ya doing, Sean?"

Instead of answering in kind, Sean grunted and motioned for Al to raise his arms. When he did, the doorman plucked Al's gun from the holster beneath his left shoulder, normally hidden by the cut of his suit, then gave him a cursory pat-down. Satisfied that Al had no other weapons, Sean nodded and placed Al's piece in his own jacket pocket, adding, "You'll—"

"Get it back when I leave, yeah. I been here plenty of times, Sean." There was no annoyance in Al's voice, just a little tiredness at the ritual. There was a time when he'd have been spared this treatment. Hell, there was a time when he'd have been having this meeting at the old man's estate instead of his "office." He realized he couldn't remember when he'd last been invited up to the boss's home.

Al turned towards Benny, motioned with two fingers spun clockwise in a small circle. Benny grimaced, but held up his arms as Al had. Sean frisked the young man, removed his weapon—carried in an extra-deep sport-coat pocket, instead of a holster—as he had Al's. He didn't bother repeating the spiel about how Benny would get it back.

Benny's lip curled upwards, then fell back into place as he straightened his clothing and joined Al on the far side of the little corridor. The room it opened onto was larger than the unassuming entrance suggested. An older part of the building, an area of the original restaurant from when it had been built nearly half a century earlier, this room had been repurposed from a small section of the old restaurant's sprawling kitchen into a place of the utmost privacy. It was separated from the current kitchen by a short hallway accessed by a recessed, nearly hidden doorway on the far side of the room, allowing its occupants service without wait-staff needing to travel through the length of the building, as Al and Benny had.

Though this area had once been part of a kitchen, such extensive remodeling had been done that it wasn't possible to even guess at its original incarnation. The room's walls were paneled in dark, finely grained wood, giving the space an intimate, warmly masculine look, while the chamber's scratched, black and white-checked tile floor — original to the building's construction — and potted fern plants lent it a nostalgic touch. These features, however, contrasted with the single sleek, expensively upholstered and modernly designed, curved leather booth, sitting on a slightly raised platform in the middle of the room, and the large-screen, high-definition, LED television mounted and hanging from the ceiling in one corner. The combined effect of the two distinct eras of design coexisting in such small quarters gave the room a slightly schizophrenic air, though no one would ever dare say that aloud to the man who sat at its center like an aging Caesar.

Al lowered his head respectfully. "Mister Castella." Alongside him, Benny mimicked the gesture, but said nothing.

The old man, his wispy, snow-white hair perfectly coifed, was clad in an exquisitely tailored, charcoal-gray suit that could do nothing to hide the unsightly folds of skin that hung from his neck, a remainder from the days when he had been called "Fat Eddie" by both friends and rivals.

Likewise, the expensive trappings could do nothing to improve the sour look on his wrinkled face as he turned towards the man seated at his left. Despite his fragile appearance, Eddie Castella's voice held strength when he spoke. "Marty, take a walk a minute, will ya? I got some things to discuss with these boys. We'll pick up our conversation shortly."

Marty Teehan, dressed casually in a yellow polo shirt and khaki slacks, was nearly of an age with his boss, but retained both a semblance of fitness and a few still-dark streaks in his otherwise gray hair. Eyes on the two newcomers, he stood without a word, then moved towards the door through which Al and Benny had entered, disappearing from sight.

"And you," Castella gestured towards a blonde young woman wearing the white shirt and black slacks of La Cucina's wait-staff, who stood in a corner of the room so quietly, so unobtrusively that Al hadn't even noticed her. "Get this shit outta here." He waved a hand at the scattered remains of a meal before him and the girl scurried forward, collecting the dishes and wine-glass with admirable speed and efficiency before disappearing through the kitchen-side doorway, on the opposite end of the room.

Settling his gaze on Al and Benny, Castella gestured curtly for them to approach, less a wave than a flap of the fingers. "Boys, c'mon up. Have a seat."

Simultaneously, each of the younger men scaled the two low, wide steps to the platform and took seats across from Castella, who watched impassively until they were settled in before asking, "Can I get you anything? A drink? Something to eat?" The words were civil, the politeness expected of a host of a gentleman from the old school that Castella had striven to be, but the tone hardly matched. Rather, it was almost chilly, as if dealing with his subordinates was distasteful, at best.

Al winced inwardly, ground his molars together to stop himself from letting it show. *Jesus. All the meals we shared in the past*, he thought. Was it just him, Al, who was the problem? Or was Castella like this with everyone else, too? In this business, not many people lived as long as Castella had and everyone, Castella included, knew it. Al wondered if it was making the old man paranoid. Maybe fear made him distrust even those, like Al, who'd been around him long enough that they should be approve reproach.

All of this flashed through his mind in an instant. Aloud, all he said was, "No, I'm good, but thank you, sir."

If Benny noticed the old mobster's manner, however, it was lost on him. "Hey, thanks, boss. I could eat."

Castella waved two fingers at the blonde waitress who had at some point silently reappeared in her corner, without even looking in her direction. "Bring somethin' for the hungry young man, would you, darling?" Apparently satisfied that his duties as host were met, Castella continued. "So, how's your night been, fellas?"

A sommelier appeared at Castella's elbow, filling a fresh wine-glass for him before offering the bottle silently to Benny and Al.

"Nothin' for me," Al declined. Benny accepted. The man poured him a glass and then disappeared as quickly and quietly as he'd arrived. As he left, the waitress returned to deposit a basket of bread and a plate of pasta before the young man. Pasta with marinara, Al noted, somehow both vaguely amused and absurdly relieved.

"Well? Don't keep me waitin'." Irritation crept into Castella's voice, but his gaze caught Al's and he added, "And don't worry about her." He jutted his chin towards the corner where the waitress had once again taken up her post. "You know as well as I do that everybody in this place is a good little boy or girl who knows what side their bread's buttered on. So go ahead."

Castella trusted the waitress, but Al, who'd worked for him for decades, needing a patting down before being admitted to his presence. Al silently grit his teeth again.

He met his boss's gaze across the table, uncomfortable now – and not only about discussing business in front of outsiders, regardless of what Castella said. Loose lips really did sink ships; Al knew that better than most. An order was an order, but he chose his words carefully all the same. "We been okay tonight, I guess, Mister Castella. 'Cept Brentano still wouldn't play ball."

Through a mouthful of bread, Benny chimed in. "Yeah, so we got a little rough."

Al's face darkened at the interjection from the young man who was, technically, his subordinate. He wanted to cuff the kid upside the head. "Uh, yeah... a lot rough, truth be told."

Castella's expression was unchanged. "So our friend Mister Brentano is...?"

"No longer an issue, per instructions."

"Well, I guess that's good to hear. I would'a rather had the money, but what are you gonna do?" Castella nodded slightly, as if the obliquely stated information didn't matter to him one way or the other. "Anyway—"

Benny cut him off: "I got a question, Mister Castella." It came out *Mist-uh Castella*, like a cable TV crime show's stereotypical mook. "If a dude owes you money, what's the point'a whackin' him? How you gonna get it then?"

"Benny!" Al gnashed his teeth and stared daggers at the youth, who gave him a "who me?" look in return as he shoveled a forkful of pasta into his mouth.

Al apologized to Castella for Benny's rudeness, but the old man surprised him with a dry chuckle. "Heh, heh, nah. It's okay, Al. We got an inquisitive mind here." He fixed his focus on Benny, still chowing down, oblivious to his lapse in etiquette. "It's all still new to the boy."

"Yeah, but..." Al trailed off.

Castella waved his objections away, eyes still trained on Benny. "Y'see kid, we were *never* gonna get that money from Mister Brentano. He had willingly entered into an arrangement, a partnership of sorts, with us—with me—and he had benefitted from that quite a bit over the last few years. So much so, I suppose, that he was feeling high and mighty enough to renege on the deal we had between us. Why he thought he'd get away with this, I couldn't say," Castella's eyes narrowed as his tone grew grave, "but that's no way to do business."

Benny's head bobbed amiably, eagerly. "Gotcha, boss."

"Do you? I hope so, because above all, our business is based on mutual trust. Trust that Salvatore Brentano broke. Walked all over it, then squatted and took a shit on it, in fact. And I tried. Believe me, I did. He was given plenty of opportunities to make right his transgression — more chances than he deserved, really — and all that came of it was that it was made clear he had no intention of giving me what was rightfully mine."

Render unto Caesar, Al thought.

Castella leaned forward on the table, putting him that much closer to his audience as he continued. "And why is that, Benny? Cuz Brentano didn't think we were serious. He thought this was an organization to be trifled with. That I was a man to whom you could break promises. That we could be used for someone else's purposes and tossed away. Well…" Castella smiled slyly. "Now he knows we're serious. Now he knows I keep *my* promises. And so do his family, and his friends and his employees and his neighbors… Not every one of those folks will know what Brentano was into. Hell, most probably have no idea. But enough of 'em will know enough about his business to get the message and then – well, you're a bright boy. You see where this is going, right?"

Benny nodded, slowly this time, as if he was actually thinking on it. Before he could say a word, however, powerful hands fell on his shoulders, gripping him lightly, but firmly. Surprised, Benny looked up to find Marty Teehan had returned. The big man's ability to move soundlessly was impressive.

"Best to always keep a firm hand on things. You get what I mean, kid?" Teehan's voice was a deep rumble over Benny's head, like thunder from an oncoming storm.

Castella's face fell back into its default expression of wrinkled disdain, his eyes flicking from Benny to Marty before coming to rest on Al for a moment. "I think he understands just fine, Marty. Well, then," he clapped his hands together, putting a cap on the discussion. "Don't let me keep you any longer, fellas. Thanks for your help tonight and you go have yourselves a pleasant evening."

Newly made or not, even Benny could tell when he had been dismissed and stood from the table, casting a brief, wistful look at his half-finished meal. "Thank you, too, Mister," *Mist-uh*, "Castella." He nodded and stepped down from the platform.

Al stood, as well. "You got it, sir. Glad to be of help. You have a nice night." He nodded respectfully, glad the conference was over, and made to join Benny at the door to the chamber, but was stopped by a hand on his arm – the same firm grasp that had pinned Benny in place moments earlier.

"A moment of your time, Al," Marty said, *sotto voce*, and guided Al to the doorway where Benny waited. "Go on ahead, Benny. Mister Vacarro will be right with you." He nodded to Sean, who walked Benny out into the hallway, and released his grip on Al only when the pair were gone.

Al shook his suit jacket's sleeve out, letting it fall back into place after the mild manhandling. His irritation was clear. He hadn't been around as long as Marty, but plenty long enough; he didn't deserve this crap.

Al shot a look over the bigger man's shoulder towards Castella, who had turned on the television hanging from the ceiling. Was that indifference studied or real?

Still, Martin Teehan was second only to Castella in the organization. No matter how brusquely he treated Al, it wouldn't do to show a lack of respect. He looked Marty in the eye when he spoke. "What's up?"

"Keep that damned kid in line." It was said quietly, calmly, but that made the menace all the more apparent. "You're on thin ice already, Al, and after what I saw back there, I thought I'd remind you that this is an obligation you want to make good on. Castella's always liked you, but he doesn't let feelings get in the way when it comes to this business. Understand?"

Al's nose crinkled at the offense, but he tamped it down. "Hey, I know my job, don't I? And I do it."

12

Marty shook his head slowly as he spoke. "Al, don't make this an issue. I don't like the kid, either, but we all have unpleasant jobs to do from time to time. You know who takes care of you and what you owe."

There were any number of answers to that. All of them raced through Al's head in the space of an instant.

He brushed them all aside and without a word, he turned and followed after Benny.

2

It wasn't even summer yet according to the calendar, but try telling that to the thermometer. Not quite noon yet, but already eighty-three degrees, humid like a sauna, and with no way to relieve it. School had let out for the year earlier in the week, so the public pool wouldn't be open for at least a few more days.

"Ahhh, it's so God-damned fuckin' hot!"

"Shut up, Mikey!" Ronnie snapped, worried blue eyes peering from over the top of the beat-up *Superman* comic he'd fished out of a trashcan in the park a few days earlier. His tone turned whiney. "My ma's upstairs with the windows open. She'll hear you."

Mike waved a hand lazily, batting away his friend's concern. "She's heard worse." Mike flashed the nasty little smile he always used when looking for trouble. "So screw her. Right, Al?"

Ronnie's face turned red, and not from the heat, but he knew better than to mess with Mike when he got like this. He looked plaintively at Al, as if saying *He's* your *cousin. Do something.*

Al shrugged and wiped at the line of sweat growing on his brow. These two always fought when they were bored. Al could hardly blame them, though. There's shit-all to do when you're ten years old and school's out, but summer hasn't yet gotten properly started. Still, the fighting would escalate if it wasn't nipped in the bud and he didn't want another lecture from Aunt Edna about "letting" Mike fight. Like it was *his* fault.

"Lay off, Mikey, will ya? It's too hot for that crap."

Mike hopped from the bottom step of the stoop, stood and stretched like a cat, drawing each muscle out to its full length and yawning. "Shit yeah, it is." He scratched at his Pink Panther t-shirt-covered belly, pretending not to watch Ronnie out of the corner of his eye, but it didn't matter – the younger boy didn't rise to the bait, keeping his nose buried in the comic instead.

"And God, I'm bored," Mike added, as if that wasn't obvious.

"So what d'ya wanna do today, then?" Al asked.

"Something to get outta this heat. We know anybody with A/C?"

Al snorted. "Yeah, right."

Ronnie piped up. "How 'bout a movie?"

"With what money, genius? It ain't free. You gonna find *that* in the trash, too?" He took a swipe at Ronnie's comic, but the boy deftly moved it aside at the last instant.

Al turned away from his friends, annoyed by the bickering, but unable to come up with any solutions himself. They always left it to him. Mike complained, Ronnie made unfeasible suggestions, and Al found the middle-ground that brought them together in the end. He didn't know why, that's just the way it had always been. But he didn't care to even go through the motions this time. He didn't want to wrack his brain in this heat or get in between the other boys' arguments. He wished something would happen, something to come along and drop a distraction in their collective lap.

And then, like magic, it did.

Down the block, from around the corner, came three men, sauntering along as if there wasn't a care in the world, dressed to the nines as if the day wasn't sweltering, wielding swagger like a weapon.

Al grinned. Ronnie and Mike's voices fell away to silence, their squabbles and boredom reduced to insignificance, pushed out of Al's consciousness by something that actually mattered. Eddie Castella hadn't been around the block in weeks, so far as Al had seen. Well, maybe when he'd been at school, but that didn't count – not in the face of hero-worship. The other guys would probably razz him about it later, but he didn't care; he couldn't help it. Growing up in the neighborhood that he did, it was only natural for Al to be fascinated by Eddie and the others. The made men. They were the coolest guys on Earth and they were well aware it.

Castella, dapper in a navy-blue, three-piece suit over a white shirt, set off by a paisley tie and bright red pocket-square, was flanked by two men: large, almost brutish-looking, but soft-spoken Martin Teehan, wearing a suit less-flamboyant than, but equally finely tailored as Castella's; and the man most familiar of the three, Tony Vacarro, Al's father, wearing a suit twin to Castella's save for being a dark green and lacking the pocket-square. Al's heart swelled with pride to see his dad walking side by side with such bigshots.

The men neared. Mike and Ronnie finally noticed and shut up, nodding respectfully, as they'd seen grownups do, as Eddie Castella passed by; Castella threw them a jaunty little salute in return. Al wanted to say something—Tony and Eddie were so close the guy was practically family—but kept mum. He was a kid, but he wasn't stupid; this was a man to whom you showed respect. You didn't just blurt out greetings like he was some everyday Joe.

Tony Vacarro, however, was another story.

"Hi, dad!"

Tony smiled, stopped, leaned against the railing of the stoop, cool even at rest. "Hiya, Alfy. Hiya, Mikey. You guys behavin'?"

"Yes, sir, Uncle Tony," Mike said quietly, answering for them both, all signs of attitude and all posturing gone. Al may have been Tony's son, but as the older of the boys, it was Mike's duty to keep his cousin safe and in line. At least when adults were watching, anyway.

16

"Not for long, I imagine, though, huh?" Tony grinned slyly. "You guys look bored and bored boys don't behave too well for too long." He reached inside his jacket.

Al could feel Ronnie, to his left and ever the worrywart, stiffen slightly.

Tony withdrew from an inside pocket a wad of cash as big as a fist and peeled off a pair of five-dollar bills, slipping them into Mike's eager, outstretched hand. "So why don't you boys get out of this heat and go see that new '*Star Wars*' movie this afternoon? And take Ronnie there with ya. I hear that flick's some kinda hot shit."

Mike turned to Al, then Ronnie, beaming and clutching the bills like the treasure they were. Ronnie looked relieved.

It's my dad, you pussy, Al thought, annoyed at his friend's skittishness. *What'd you think was gonna happen?*

"Thanks, dad," he said. Tony smiled and ruffled his son's crewcut.

"Hey, Tony, c'mon. You wanna be the one keepin' my pop waitin'?"

Tony's head turned. "Comin', Eddie." And his body followed his gaze an instant later, hurrying to catch up to the other men, tossing a wave over his shoulder to his son and nephew and their friend. "See ya at dinner, Alfy; don't be late. And you be sure to tell me how the movie is, okay?"

Al watched the three men who, though few said it out loud, ruled the neighborhood as they disappeared around the far corner at the end of the block. There was a thought tickling the outer edges of his mind, but it remained unformed as Mike interrupted him with a slap on the back, then bolted down the sidewalk in the direction Tony and company had come from.

"Race ya to the theater, suckers!" Mike laughed.

"It's on!" Ronnie hopped up and gave chase, his precious, found comic left behind on the concrete steps, forgotten at the prospect of a free movie and relief from the heat. "Ain't no contest between you and me, Mike! C'mon, Al!"

Al shot a last look up the street towards where the men had gone. Something continued to nag at the back of his mind, struggling to rise through thoughts of popcorn and spaceships, as he stepped down from the stoop and followed his friends at a more sedate pace. Those men, his father and Castella and even Teehan—the mick among wops as Mike had called him once, earning a cuff and a lecture from Aunt Edna—they didn't just run these blocks and neighborhoods like a business, like their own fiefdom – they were *from* here. Same as Al, same as Mike and Ronnie and all their friends. Same history, same values, same *blood*. The boys didn't know what their fathers, uncles and brothers did, exactly, only that it was *business*, nebulous, but all-important and that it was theirs and someday, it would be Al's and his friends', too.

"Hey, Al! Last one's a rotten egg, you know!"

Al didn't respond, but hurried his pace all the same. Deep thoughts or no, nobody wanted to be the rotten egg – and besides, what did it matter what dad and Eddie Castella and the others did for a living? Al knew who took care of him, and when you're ten years old, that's all that matters.

3

Outside the restaurant, the cool night air did little to sooth Al's smoldering irritation.

"Keep that damned kid in line."

How? With a fucking muzzle? Al could show Benny the ropes, make sure the day's assignments got done, but controlling what flew out of his mouth would require the hand of God. Pulling the kid into this business, this life, wasn't his idea. But now it was his responsibility to settle him into it? At one time, it might have been a sign of trust, of confidence in Al's abilities and his position in the organization; bringing up the next generation was important, he couldn't deny that. But this didn't seem like that. Not at all. It seemed like punishment. For what, he couldn't say, but it felt like further evidence of a growing rift between himself and Castella, a man he'd once idolized.

"'S'about time, man." Al turned towards the voice, spotting the amber glow of a cigarette in the semi-darkness before he saw Benny himself, leaning against the red-brick exterior of the building, just outside the range of the lights over the entrance. "What'd Teehan want?"

19

Al ignored him and started towards the corner and the parking lot beyond, stepping out of the light and moving past Benny. The younger man grinned around his smoke and added, "He give you a little spankin' for not gettin' Castella's money from that stiff, Brentano?"

Still within arm's reach of the kid, Al gritted his teeth, snatched the cigarette from Benny's stupid, smirking mouth and tossed it away, little sparks marking its passage as it flipped end over end through the darkness.

Benny's amusement disappeared in an instant, replaced by confusion and annoyance. "Hey, what the fuck?"

The kid's confusion was warranted, but his complaining sounded like nothing more than petulance compared to Al's own concerns.

"Christ," Al shook his head, a thousand different responses on his tongue. He chose: "There really must be something wrong with you." He turned the corner and continued towards his car, footsteps slapping softly against the faded, cracked blacktop of the parking lot, competing with the faint sounds of conversation coming from a car parked kitty-corner to the lot's entrance. Somewhere in the distance, from the direction of one of the city's main thoroughfares, a car honked its horn angrily and repeatedly.

Left behind, mouth agape, Benny cocked his head like a perplexed animal and stared at Al's retreating back. "What? Where the hell's that comin' from? Hey, wait up!"

Al had no intention of leaving without Benny. Abandoning him would be more trouble than it was worth, and he didn't need any more trouble tonight. Car-keys in hand, he looked across the roof of the Crown Vic at Benny as the other man trotted up to the vehicle. "Benny," Al said. "Let me ask you: are you fucking stupid or something?"

Benny's eyes blazed as an acidic retort formed on his lips, but Al continued, preempting Benny's reply with a short, curt wave of the hand, adding, "You don't *ever* question Mister Castella about *anything*." He stuck his key in the car door, opened it, and slid in before leaning over to unlock the passenger's door for Benny.

Benny considered options and responses for a moment, anger burning at his brain and in his cheeks. Who gave Al the right to order him around?

Shit, he realized. *The old man did.*

He got into the car without a word.

Al started the car, buckled up and flicked on the headlights. He took a slow breath through his nose before turning towards Benny. The edge was gone from his voice when he said, "And don't worry what other people are talkin' about. You'll be told if you need to know, you understand? Remember what Castella said?" he continued. "That this business is all about respect? Well, that's only half of it: a big part is discretion, too. You remember both of 'em, you hear me?"

He put the car into reverse and added to himself, *He's young and dumb and it's all new to him, like Castella said, but shit... was I ever this fuckin' mouthy or arrogant?* He hoped to God not. He couldn't bear the thought.

Benny's lips moved, as if repeating the words, trying to work out the shape of what Al had said, then he nodded. He realized what Al said was true, even if he didn't like being told. "Hey, uh, Al," he ventured. "I get you, but the boss seemed okay with it. He said I got an inquisitive mind and all... that's good, right?"

Al put the car back into park and placed his head against the steering wheel, all in one motion. "Christ, you *are* stupid!" he cried, but the tone was lighter this time and he tilted his head sideways enough to flash Benny a little grin.

Benny grinned back, message received. "Okay, so maybe I am a little bit. I'll try to watch my big mouth better."

Al nodded, shifted the car back into gear and pointed the vehicle towards the street. "Good. That's all I'm saying, you know?"

"So, hey," Benny started, changing the subject, "the night's still young. You wanna hit the club?"

"Yeah, okay... relaxing a little before headin' home sounds good. But seriously," he threw Benny a meaningful look. "Just go along in the future. Do what you're told, no questions. Questions can easily become problems."

So can people, Benny thought, somewhere in the back of his mind.

***

The car rolled to a gentle stop before a sign indicating VIP parking, the hood reflecting the glow of three-foot tall neon lights spelling out "Bottoms Up", the *m* cleverly made to resemble a woman's rear-end. In smaller letters beneath the neon, a painted sign unnecessarily clarified: "A gentlemen's club". Various other signs, touting virtues such as live dancers and cold beer, added to the effect, but could do nothing to conceal the fact that the structure still strongly resembled the pizza chain-restaurant it had begun life as sometime in the nineteen-eighties. It somehow seemed bizarrely funny to Al and he had always gotten as big a kick out of that as he did the place's current offerings – well, almost as big a kick.

"Hell, yeah," Benny half-whispered, his eyes lighting up with glee as he unbuckled his seatbelt.

"Been a while?" Al asked.

"Yeah, since last night!" Benny cackled. His smile turned wicked as he added, "Hey, you got a girl here, right?"

"Right," Al said and slid from the car.

The club's double, glass and metal exterior doors were unattended but inside a second "door" of thickly strung, hanging beads obstructed views of the interior. It was flanked by signs indicating minors were prohibited entry and instructing patrons to have IDs at the ready. Benny ignored these and pushed through the hangings with a wide, lustful leer, calling out, "Hellllooo, ladies!" as he did, only to walk smack into a third wall of broad, t-shirt-clad flesh.

"Yo, cover."

Leer gone, replaced by a look of confused indignation, Benny stared at the hand on his chest. He looked up into the impassive, almost bored-seeming, face of a muscular black man who stood at least a head and a

22

half taller than himself. Bald-headed, but impressively bearded to make up for it, the man wore a black t-shirt, emblazoned with the word "SECURITY", that contrasted with his milk-chocolate skin, but matched the onyx chips of his eyes, set under a heavy brow. Al didn't recognize the man, but that wasn't unusual. Turnover was high at a place like this. He hoped Benny would take this minor interruption to his evening in stride, especially as the bouncer looked like he could toss the much smaller man out on his ear without breaking a sweat.

Size and muscle-mass, however, were no deterrent in the face of tits or stupidity. Benny snapped, "What the fuck is this?!" and slapped the hand away from his chest.

Without missing a beat or breaking his expressionless mask, the man raised a hand towards the door. "Ten dollar cover, man. It's posted." He gestured toward a sign indicating as much to the left of the entrance. "Both outside and in. Pony up or take a hike."

That was exactly the right response. Al hid his smile, admiring the man's restraint and professionalism. He liked this new guy; it took a firm, dispassionate hand to run security at a place like this. A hothead at the door wasn't good for anyone. And Al didn't mind seeing Benny get his nose rubbed in it a little bit, either.

Benny was less impressed and he obviously didn't share in the opinion. He balled a fist in front of his chest and snarled, "Are you fucking kidding me? You God-damned—" He caught himself before saying something he couldn't take back. He changed tacks: "You know who I am?!"

"Benny." Al put a hand on the angry youth's shoulder, the tension in Benny's muscles evident through the thin material of his cheap, white suit jacket. "Shut the fuck up a sec, will ya?" Al caught the bouncer's eye over Benny's shoulder. "We're personal guests of Mister Castella."

The man's expression cracked for a second, allowing indecision to peek through from behind his professionally blank face. He shook his head slightly. "Mister Castella ain't in tonight."

Al let out a sound half-groan, half-sigh. The guy was trying to do his job, but c'mon. His opinion of the man slipped a tiny bit. "You must be new, but you don't look stupid, so maybe think about that for a minute."

Evidently, the man did and a moment was all it took. His entire manner changed, becoming solicitous – almost overly so. "Shit, I didn't know." His head bobbed in contrition and he stepped aside, waving for the pair to enter. "I'm sorry, fellas. Really, I am. Go right on in."

Al nodded in return and rewarded the man with a gracious smile, magnanimous in victory. "'S'okay, no harm done. Now you've seen our faces and you'll remember next time."

Benny sneered in disdain and straightened his jacket as he strutted forward, brushing past the big man as if he was invisible, ignoring his apparently sincere apology. "Who the hell does he think he is, that uppity—"

"I told you, shut the fuck up. Keep your comments to yourself," Al stage-whispered, administering a sharp elbow to Benny's back, cutting the insult short and prodding him forward.

The altercation by the entrance had given Al's eyes plenty of time to adjust to the club's dimly-lit interior. He took the lead, guiding Benny through an atmosphere of smoke and hard rock music so loud and distorted it was little more than noise, past postage-stamp-sized tables, occupied by individuals or small groups. Every single customer was male.

Weaving around nearly nude waitresses bearing trays loaded with pint- and shot-glasses, the pair headed towards the tiny VIP area at the rear of the dark, crowded space. Separated from the rest of the club by a threadbare velvet rope, the area was special in name only, but did offer unobstructed views of the main stage, tinsel-strewn and neon-drenched, where a dead-eyed, topless brunette swung listlessly from a pole, backed by her own reflection gleaming from half a dozen floor-to-ceiling mirrors at the rear of the stage.

Signaling a waitress who nodded that she saw him, but didn't interrupt her progress towards the back wall where the bar was located, Al sat and motioned for Benny to do the same. "Have a drink, relax and for the love of God, *behave.*"

Al had to practically shout over the music and wasn't sure Benny heard him even then. The younger man didn't respond, his eyes glued to the woman on the stage, now a little more energetic as the music changed from rock to some hip-hop song with a pulsating bass line – apparently more her speed. She gyrated her hips and pressed her smallish tits against the steel pole with something approaching enthusiasm. Benny's eyes and grin both widened in appreciation.

"Hey!" Al snapped. "Listen up! I'm serious here. This is a legitimate business." As legitimate as a strip club could be, at any rate. "So don't cause any more scenes or any trouble for Mister Castella. What the fuck did I say about discretion?"

Benny nodded, but didn't still reply, preoccupied with the sight of the writhing girl, his eyes focused like lasers and his tongue pressed between his teeth in a way that was both obscene and vaguely disquieting.

Al stood, fists against the table as if pushing himself to his feet. "Whatever. I'll be back later."

He stopped the waitress he'd signaled before, placing an order on Benny's behalf for a cheap, domestic beer and then headed through a door off to one side of the bar. Through an almost-entirely darkened corridor leading into the depths of the building, he passed beyond the areas that most patrons would ever see, stopping before a nondescript door.

Knocking softly, he called, "Jenna! You there?"

"Who is it?" a high, girlish voice from behind the door asked.

Al rolled his eyes, unwilling to play this game after the night he'd already had. "Who d'you think it is?"

The door cracked open wide enough to reveal a slate-gray eye, set off by smoky-green eyeshadow. "Al?"

Annoyed, Al said, "You see it's me, don't ya?"

The door flew open and a lithe but curvy blonde, wearing a short diaphanous robe that hid nothing, nearly leapt into Al's arms, throwing her own around his neck and pressing her lips to his, tongue snaking between his teeth, sharing the taste of cigarettes and mint lip-balm. Al let the kiss linger a moment then pulled back. The girl gave him a teasing smile. "Why didn't you say so in the first place, baby?"

Al licked his lips, savoring the flavor of the bold, brassy, little woman. The kiss had been brief, but fierce; it was exactly what he needed. He smiled back and pushed her gently into the small, dingy room. Even in the depths of the building, he could clearly hear the music from the main room, but at least he didn't have to shout to be heard. "Why? Who else comes lookin' for you this time of night?"

Jenna's smile turned wicked as she closed the door behind her and moved towards a makeup table at the far end of the little room, rear-end twitching enticingly beneath the thin fabric of the robe. "You'd be surprised." She opened the bottom drawer and lifted out a bottle of whiskey and a mismatched pair of glasses.

The kiss, and really, just seeing Jenna, had improved Al's mood considerably. He settled into a well-worn easy chair by the window, sealed haphazardly against the night with bent and dusty venetian blinds. He decided he'd play along a little, after all. "So you got other guys comin' around here, huh?"

Jenna filled one glass with amber liquid before turning and handing it to Al, giving him a wink. "Why not? 'S'not like I'm your only woman, right?"

The good mood Al had been cultivating vanished. His face grew dark and his expression closed off. Quietly, in a near-monotone, he said, "You shut your God damned mouth about that. You know it pisses me right the fuck off."

Jenna knew – and she knew when not to push. She adjusted her tone accordingly. "Oh, Alfy…" she cooed, settling herself lightly on Al's lap, her toned, bronzed legs dangling over one side of the chair. She tousled his thinning, graying hair. "I'm sorry. I was only teasing a little. I didn't mean nothing by it." She buried her face in his neck, nuzzling him softly.

"And don't call me 'Alfy.' It's 'Al,' you got it? I'm not some damned kid." Al tossed back half of the almost-forgotten whiskey. He grunted, feeling the liquor burn its way down his throat, then spread through his belly. He cleared his throat against the liquor's heat before continuing. "I hate that name, 'Alfonse.'"

Jenna ran gentle fingers across Al's cheek, smiling coyly, sweetly, almost shyly. "Why? I like it. I think it's cute."

Even as keyed up as he was from the past couple of hours, Al's anger was no match for Jenna's loving ministrations. He still wasn't quite ready to let it go, though. He gulped down the remainder of the glass's contents. "You and my mother both."

"C'mere." Jenna pulled Al's face to hers, using his tie like a leash, and kissed him softly.

He broke off and pulled back, giving himself room to set the empty glass on the floor and freeing a hand to gently cup the back of her head, pulling her close again for a kiss, while settling her firm, curvy butt over his rapidly stiffening crotch.

Jenna giggled and wriggled her hips, grinding herself against him. "There's someone who can't stay mad at me for long."

Al grinned and shifted Jenna forward again, onto his knees, giving himself enough room to shrug out of his jacket.

Jenna popped nimbly up from his lap, her dancer's skills evident in the sleek efficiency of the movement. No matter what anyone said, she was a *dancer* not a stripper. It wasn't just something she told herself, either.

"Lemme do it." She helped him remove the coat, then unstrap and unsling the holster riding beneath his shoulder. She slid the knot of his tie down enough to pull it over his head, tossing all three onto the nearby loveseat, mismatched to the chair but equally ratty. She stood over him, hands on hips, and when she made no move to return to the chair, Al looked up at her expectantly. She waggled a finger at him. "Shirt, too, mister."

Al unbuttoned the fine silk shirt carefully as Jenna climbed back into the chair – but behind him this time, pushing him forward with her knees so he had to sit on the very edge of the cushion to make room for her. With strong, practiced fingers, the woman kneaded and massaged the muscles of his upper back and shoulders. "You're so stressed tonight, baby. It's all built up back here like knots in a rope. You have a bad day?"

Al sighed, half-relaxation at her touch, half-exasperation at thoughts of the night's events. "No," he said quickly. Then, more slowly, "Well… kinda. Yeah, I guess," he finally admitted.

Jenna switched from hands to an elbow, working at a tight little bunch of muscles along Al's shoulder-blade. "Somethin' you can talk about? I'm always happy to listen."

Al groaned, all pleasure this time. Even without her other talents and assets, Jenna's hands alone made her worth her weight in gold as far as he was concerned. "Not a word to anyone else, but… it's Benny. That kid's getting wild." He blew air and shook his head.

Jenna hadn't met Benny, but she'd heard the name often enough the last few weeks. She switched back to using her hands, a practiced palm kneading Al's flesh like dough, working out the iron-hard stress as she tried to get him to talk out the cause. "What do you mean?"

Al closed his eyes and took a deep breath through his mouth, releasing it through his nose slowly, enjoying the massage and trying to decide how much he could tell Jenna. He'd warned Benny about talking out of turn, hadn't he? But Jenna was a good girl. She was *his* girl. And who else could he talk to about this kind of thing?

Al grunted as Jenna hit a sore spot near his spine. "To the left," he directed, then, "The kid's less than a month into this job and he hasn't really learned shit, but he thinks he knows it all."

Jenna had heard this line before. "But that's what kids are like, right?"

Al snorted. "I call him a 'kid' — hell, everyone does far as I can tell — but he's God-damned twenty-four years old. That's a man where I'm from." He sighed. "But yeah, I guess these days, that is still a kid, ain't it?"

Jenna was twenty-three. She wondered, what did that make her?

Al paused. So did Jenna, hands resting motionless on Al's broad back, palms pressed against the warm, rough skin, waiting for him to finish. Finally, "This whole thing is going to his head. He thinks it's all a game. He thinks he's got how it's played down pat and there's nothing more anyone can teach him. He only seems to like the parts that everyone else is smart enough to stay the hell away from as much as possible. I mean... I don't know. Right from the get-go, he didn't impress me too much but now he's getting wild and I'm worried like hell over it."

Jenna crawled out from behind Al, allowing him to settle back into depths of the chair. She kneeled down in front of him and took his hands in hers. She looked up but he wouldn't meet her gaze. She let that go, but asked, "Why?" This openness, half-hearted as it was, embarrassed Al, she was aware of that – but she also that sometimes, he needed to talk whether he would admit it or not. "Why so worried, baby?" she pressed.

"Because," Al said, softly. "He's gonna fuck up and he's gonna take someone down with him and the way things are going, it's probably gonna be me."

Jenna didn't know what to say to that, what words might relieve Al of his worries. This wasn't like the stress held in his body – there were no obvious places to massage away the tension. It pained her in a way she wouldn't have been able to express if asked to, but it was there all the same.

Al cleared his throat, pretending to cough to hide his embarrassment. "Anyway, why are we talkin' about this shit?" He stood and undid his belt buckle, then his fly, letting his pants fall to pool around his ankles, before sitting back down. "That's not why I came here," he added, his tone harsher than he'd intended.

"Okay, baby." Jenna lowered her gaze. "I just wanted to help," she added quietly and if Al noticed the hurt in her voice, he pretended not to as she fished a hand into his boxer shorts.

Wrong again, Jenna, she thought, burying her face in Al's lap. *Guess there's always an obvious place.*

4

Al caught Jenna's eye over his reflection's shoulder as he stood before the mirror, putting his tie back in place. "So, I'll call you tomorrow afternoon, okay?"

Jenna's gaze darkened beneath plucked-thin eyebrows as she broke the eye-contact and flopped into the ragged easy-chair. Effortlessly, she worked her expression into a good pout—it was easy when you felt it—and reached down to the forgotten liquor bottle by the base of the chair, fingers toying with the neck of the bottle. Imagining it was something else, she squeezed the lip hard enough to make the tips of her fingers ache, wishing for a moment she could make Al hurt, even a little bit. The feeling would pass, but maybe not so quickly as it once might have.

"Can't you stay with me tonight?" she asked. "Just this once? We could go back to my place…" She tried to turn her pout into the sexy kind, but if Al saw it in the mirror, the effort was ignored.

Al turned, his face expressionless, and took a step towards the chair where Jenna perched. Her heart leapt in her chest so powerfully it hurt – but came crashing back down even harder when Al leaned past her to pluck his suit-jacket from where it had somehow ended up draped across the back of the seat.

"Don't start," he said, his voice flat, but anger flashing in his eyes. "You know what this is."

There was a burning in her own eyes, then an uncomfortable tingle at the corner of each of eye, as Al turned back towards the mirror and shrugged the jacket on in the same motion. He shook out the cuffs of his sleeves, then brushed them out with his hands. He stuffed his tie into the outside pocket of his jacket, then picked up the holstered Browning, wrapped the narrow, elastic shoulder-straps around the holster and shoved the bundle into the jacket's inner pocket. It would bulge pretty badly, but nobody in the club would be paying him any attention.

No one but Jenna. Her eyes absorbed every little movement as she grabbed up the bottle she'd been fingering and took a choking gulp, trying to crush one burn with another.

She swallowed hard before finally responding, "Yeah... I know."

Al took another look at himself in the mirror, smoothed down the jacket's lapels, ran fingers through his hair and nodded, satisfied that he looked presentable and that there was no evidence of the previous hour's activities. He stepped towards the chair one final time, leaning down for a kiss, but Jenna twisted around to face the wall, showing him her back.

Al clenched his teeth sharply, biting back even sharper words.

Sick of this shit, he thought. His good mood upon first seeing Jenna was evaporating as quickly as it first grew. The talking, the admissions he'd made, had embarrassed and frustrated him and even what they'd done afterwards hadn't helped. Now the time felt wasted, lost. "Fine, be that way," he snapped, adding, "I'll *still* call you tomorrow."

Jenna listened to his footsteps, rapid and heavy across the scarred tiled floor, and when the door clicked open, then slammed shut an instant later, she let out the breath she hadn't realized she'd been holding, letting the tears that she'd been fighting back flow freely.

***

On the other side of the door, Al heard none of Jenna's soft sobs, only the pulsating bass coming from the main part of the club and an assortment of muted squeals, giggles and moans from behind several of the other doors that lined the hallway. The familiar space felt uncomfortably close and dark. He had a sudden, desperate urge to escape.

Jenna had been getting needy lately. The last two years with her had been good — great at times — but maybe it was time to put an end to this thing. Do it like a Band-Aid, one clean tearing motion, one painful moment and then over and done with. He almost reached for the doorknob again, but stopped, shook his head. He didn't have the mental energy left to deal with this tonight. He turned on his heel and headed back out into the club proper.

Back in the main room, the thumping bass line had shifted into the raucous screams of competing electric guitars as a girl he'd never seen before strutted out onto the glittering, neon-bathed stage, all long legs, plastic breasts and bucktoothed grin. From overhead, the club's DJ announced the girl, but Al couldn't make out much, the club-host's voice nearly lost amidst the catcalls and whoops that went up from the crowd nearest the stage. As the girl hip-swung her way back and forth across the length of the small platform, joined by a small army of identical girls marching in the mirrors behind her, she threw little waves and kisses to the men lined up along its edges, basking in the glow of momentary stardom. It had been a while since Al had seen a girl up there who looked like she wanted to be; he wondered how long it would last.

Al's eyes moved from the young woman to the crowd of her fans, searching for Benny. He had no idea what time it was, but the night seemed to have lasted days already. He wanted nothing more than to head home, but he and Benny had arrived together and leaving without even checking in with the kid would cause problems later. He hated to even imagine the whining he'd have to endure the next day if Benny thought he'd been ditched.

Turning from the stage, Al scanned the rest of the dimly-lit space, finally spotting Benny in one of the far corners. He headed in that direction but, midway across the room, stopped in his tracks when he realized Benny wasn't alone. Half-hidden in the shadows of the slight recess, the other man was getting a lap-dance from the floppy-titted, dead-eyed brunette they'd seen on stage earlier. The girl, topless but still wearing her G-string, listlessly ground herself against Benny's crotch and chest, ignoring the beat and rhythm of the music, making the "dancing" part debatable. Al's lip curled in disdain as Benny tilted his head back and laughed raucously, eyes gleaming darkly in the low light. He looked like he was in heaven.

Al shook his head slightly, biting back his disgust, wondering why Benny didn't at least take the girl into one of the "champagne" rooms. What the hell had he told the kid about behaving? About keeping a low profile? Did he not even know what the word "discretion" meant? Hell, it was possible. Why the fuck had he wasted the time or breath on that conversation in the car?

And then a thought struck him: *Is this what me and Jenna look like?*

He was always careful, rarely taking the girl out in public, never bragging the way some guys did about their side-pieces. He didn't flaunt the relationship, but it wasn't a complete secret, either. There were people here at the club who knew, that was unavoidable, but the two of them would never carry on with an audience like Benny. Al kept his private life private, and Jenna was smart enough to do the same, but still…

Anger and shame flared hot in Al's brain, but he shook it off, pushing the thought aside as he squared his shoulders and headed towards Benny and the girl.

Keeping several feet's distance—less from respect than disgust—Al shouted over the music, "Hey, Benny! I'm outta here. You wanna ride?"

Without sparing even a glance for Al, Benny answered, "Nah, I'm good here." He gripped the stripper by the hips, shifting her more directly onto his clearly engorged member, painfully noticeable through his already-tight pants.

Al turned on his heel, tossing a little wave over his shoulder, saying a silent thanks to whatever passed for God, glad for this minor stroke of fortune. "Suit yourself," he said, adding, "And try to keep it in your pants."

***

Outside the club, away from the glaring neon and throbbing music, the night was quiet. With the windows of the Crown Victoria down, the night's still-warm air blasting his face and roaring past his eardrums, Al felt distance growing between himself and the last several hours' events. Alone in the car, headlights streaming over miles of cracked blacktop and fading yellow lines, Al imagined he was in some sort of fast-moving cocoon, transforming the hardened, aging gangster into something else entirely as he headed towards the suburbs beyond the outskirts of the city. It was a conscious effort, one he took great, daily pains to make. The life he lived outside of his home was never to enter it, no matter what, nor could his wife or kids ever learn anything about it. His father, who'd gotten him into this thing, had made that mistake with Al and his mother. It didn't keep Al from living this life, but he'd learned the lesson his father hadn't. Keeping his two worlds separate was the one absolute law Al lived by and he put more effort into it than virtually anything else he did – in either of his lives.

The highway exit appeared all too soon, forcing Al out of his moment of Zen and, shortly, the car was turning down a sleepy cul-de-sac, crawling past tidy houses with neatly trimmed lawns and slumbering residents. It was a nice neighborhood, one it took money to live in. The residents here weren't rich, but it was a solid, upper-middle-class enclave where people worked hard for what they had and took pride in what they'd built for themselves. Al pulled the vehicle into the driveway of a pale-yellow, two-story bungalow where a lighted porch greeted him and two still-lit windows showed that someone was still awake within.

Al forced the last of the day's events from his mind, packing away "working Al," as he thought of his other life, behind mental partitions. He locked his weapon in the glove box, then exited the vehicle, shutting the car door as quietly as possible. He moved up onto the porch and entered the house. Dropping his keys into the little basket sitting on the long, wooden table against the wall inside the doorway, he spotted the flood of light from the kitchen, down the hallway that led further into the house. He stepped lightly that way, calling softly, "I'm home."

"Hi," came the reply from the kitchen.

Al stepped into the mellow, white glow of the small kitchen's overhead lighting, stopping in the arching doorway. "Lexi? Hey."

"Hey, yourself." Lexi, his wife, smiled faintly as she poured hot water from a steaming pot into a delicate-looking porcelain teacup. She dropped a small, transparent paper bag into the cup and asked, "Want some? It's called 'Sleepy-time'. I just bought it today. Supposed to be great for relaxing." She held the steeping cup of tea out towards Al.

Under the warmth of the soft lighting, Lexi almost looked like the beauty queen she once could have been, even in the worn-out, pastel-colored robe she wore over her pajamas. Blonde, full-figured and curvy, with a smile that was both mischievous and generously given, Lexi threw a then much-younger Al for a loop when they first met. He'd never known it was possible to love someone the way he had her. It was a love that hits you like a bullet: sudden, unexpected and life-changing.

Twenty some-odd years later, he still loved her, but it wasn't the same. She had grown softer and more tired; he had grown harder and more restless. A faint stickiness in his undershorts and a sudden twist of ice in his guts reminded him of that. Shame, anger and self-loathing flared; he hoped the lighting hid the faint burn he felt growing in his cheeks.

Lexi still held the steaming cup towards Al, eyes searching for contact with his.

"It's late," was all he said, as if that was an answer to her question.

Lexi shrugged and turned towards the kitchen counter, set the teacup down, removed the lid from the jar marked "SUGAR" on the counter. "How was work?" she asked.

"Work was work. The kids still up?"

Used to the brusqueness, she no longer took it personally, instead taking her time in preparing for herself the tea that Al had rebuffed. She removed the tea bag then added minute amounts of sugar and dry creamer, stirred gently, slowly, before puffing on the steaming liquid, allowing herself the luxury of perfecting this single cup. At last she sipped, deemed the new tea satisfactory with a small, pleased sigh and said, finally, "Kyle's asleep, but I think Beth is still up, reading."

Al nodded and exited the room, already headed towards the stairs at the front of the house as he tossed over his shoulder, "I guess I'll go say goodnight, then."

Lexi said nothing, just sipped her tea.

***

Upstairs, Al knocked on the first door to the left of the landing, the one marked "BETH" written out in sparkly letters and surrounded by childish drawings of unicorns and other fantasy creatures that Al couldn't identify and didn't care to try. Without waiting for a response, he entered the room, calling out quietly, "Still awake in here?"

"Daddy!" ten-year-old Beth cried, dropping the book she'd been reading as she leapt from the twin bed at the sight of him.

Al scooped the girl up as if her weight was nothing, hugging his daughter closely to his chest, feeling the flutter of her tiny heart against his, relishing the faint scent of shampoo wafting from her short, straight chestnut hair. A smile of genuine joy spread across his face. He kissed her forehead, then both cheeks, then the tip of her nose for good measure. "Hey, princess."

Beth was delighted, sighing contentedly, nuzzling her father's chin with her head. "I'm glad you're here." She looked up into his eyes, putting on a little pout. "I waited up for you, but I was getting really sleepy."

Al sat down on the edge of the small bed, scooting backwards, ruffling the princess-pink comforter, until his back was against the *Harry Potter* poster adorning the wall. "That's sweet, kiddo." Al tousled the girl's hair, relishing its silkiness, as she snuggled into his shoulder, trying to hide a yawn. "But you shouldn't stay up too late, especially not for me," he added. "You need a lotta rest to grow up big and strong."

"Aw, daddy! I *had* to!" Beth's voice grew husky and her tone became semi-accusatory. "I haven't seen you at all this week."

The girl's father sighed and eased her off of his lap until she sat next to him on the bed, one heavy arm wrapped lightly around her thin shoulders, pulling her tight against his side. "I know, princess. I'm sorry. I been workin' a lot this week."

"Dad...?" Beth ventured hesitantly.

"Yeah, sweetheart?" he answered distractedly, glancing down, his eyes sliding across the covers of the books that lay in a small, haphazard pile near his feet. Some titles he vaguely remembered from his own long-ago childhood, like *Where the Red Fern Grows* and *Charlotte's Web*. Most were more recent. *Harry Potter* he was familiar with from a few rare family movie nights. Several from a series, apparently called *Warriors*, had cats on all the covers. All of the books looked to have fallen off of the girl's narrow nightstand, though how long ago was anyone's guess. Al was proud of his daughter the reader, glad she'd taken to education and literature in a way he never had, but her tidiness needed some work. He leaned down and began to straighten the books himself.

"Where *do* you work, anyway? You've never said." Beth asked.

That got his attention. He sat ramrod straight for a moment, then shrugged elaborately for the girl's benefit and finished tidying the books, placing them on the bedside table; there was barely enough room for the dozen or so paperbacks, stacked into two orderly piles. "Uh, 'course I have. Anyway, it's time for sleep, kiddo. It's real late."

"Nuh uh." Beth crossed her arms defiantly, giving Al a commanding look – the kind designed to pin men in place. The kind that many adult women would have had to practice to perfect. It seemed to come naturally to the girl. "You've never said. Not once. I know all my friends' dads' jobs, but not yours. How come?"

Al Vacarro carried business cards that read:

Al Vacarro
Vice President of Operations
Castella Shipping & Transport

It was a lofty title in a legitimate business that Eddie Castella owned. A business that, Al understood, made a steady, if not exactly extravagant, profit. If anyone from a position of authority—cops or tax collectors, for example—came around the trucking company's offices asking after Al, they'd receive confirmation that he worked there and had for many years – he simply wasn't in the office at the moment. They didn't need to know that he would likely never be – or that he hadn't set foot inside the place in nearly six years. Al's entire paper-trail of a career was just that – it didn't exist outside of the paper it was printed on. It was a well-constructed fiction that would hold up under detailed scrutiny. And it had on more than one occasion. Only the dumbest, low-rent crooks could forget that Al Capone was taken down by the Internal Revenue Service. Subsequent generations of organized criminals learned well from the example set by Al's namesake. No matter what Al Vacarro really did to earn his pay, employment in a straight job of some sort was necessary to have any sort of life worth living and this arrangement suited Al fine: it required no upkeep or effort on his part and paychecks were deposited to his checking account every two weeks like clockwork. The system worked so well that it was hardly even a lie anymore; his employer was legitimately Castella Shipping & Transport, of which Eddie Castella was owner, president and CEO. If anyone else asked him, Al wouldn't have hesitated to answer and tell them exactly that, because it was true, to a certain, specific definition of the word. Even Lexi believed her husband worked for the shipping company.

But Beth wasn't just anyone and Al did hesitate. He'd made a lot of mistakes, both with Lexi and with the kids, over the years. Too many to count – too many to ever really make up for if he was brutally honest with himself. He preferred not to add to that list by lying to the girl, unless it was absolutely necessary. And he could almost convince himself that it wasn't a lie if he simply said nothing at all.

"Nah, I'm sure I told ya. Besides, it's boring stuff that you don't really wanna hear about," Al said with forced casualness. He picked up the book Beth had been reading when he'd entered from where it had fallen onto the bed, held it up between them. "So what's this, sweet-pea?"

"It's a book about dragons and knights," Beth answered, hurt evident in her voice. "It's really good," she added.

"Oh, yeah?"

"Yeah… but you really never told me what you do." Beth refused to be derailed. Al mentally groaned.

"Why not?" the girl continued, expression shifting freely between hurt and anger. "What am I supposed to tell my class when everyone talks about their parents' jobs on career day next week? Mom doesn't work, so it's just you and I don't even *know*," she finished, her tone edging towards shrill on the last word.

"Sure, your mom works," Al gently chided her. "Being a mom is a big deal. Most important job in the world."

"Fine," Beth pouted. "But I'm not talking about that at school!"

Al gently pushed his daughter back onto the bed, pulling the covers up over her. "Well, you like knights and dragons, right? Then you tell the kids in your class that your dad is a business knight who slays economic dragons. How 'bout that?"

Without waiting for her to respond, Al kissed Beth on the forehead, reaching out a hand to click off the bedside lamp as he did. "'Night, princess. Go to sleep now."

***

Al quietly opened the door next to Beth's and looked in on seven-year-old Kyle. He was pleased to see the child sleeping soundly, sprawled beneath the covers, one small foot protruding from beneath them. He loved both of his kids fiercely, but he had to admit that Kyle was the easy one – he never questioned or pouted or argued like Beth. He simply enjoyed the time he got with his father and took Al's frequent absences as simply another part of life. On darker nights, the boy's easy acceptance haunted Al in a way he couldn't quite wrap his head around. Kyle's lack of upset was somehow worse than Beth's guilt-trips.

Tonight, Al just smiled at the blissfully sleeping child, blew a kiss towards the boy and whispered, "Sleep tight, son."

The door closed again with a soft click and Al turned down the hallway, towards his own bedroom, moving past a wall of framed family photos, the most recent from Kyle's fourth birthday party. At the rear of the house, facing away from the street, the room was almost pitch black even with the blinds still open. Al had lived in this house, slept in this room, for nearly fourteen years, though, and day or night, the layout never changed. He ignored the light-switch on the wall, closed the blinds and began to undress.

"They really miss you, Al," Lexi said from the doorway. Her ability to move silently had always impressed, but no longer surprised, him.

Al sighed, but didn't bother turning to face her. In the darkness it didn't matter. "Yeah." He hung his jacket on a wire hanger, then placed it in the closet among half a dozen others. "I'm sorry, but work is work."

"We hardly ever see you anymore, Al." Lexi moved closer, reaching out a hand towards her husband – a darker spot in the blackness of the room. Al deftly avoided the contact, moving away from the closet and to the neatly made, king-sized bed, still not sparing Lexi a look. She wasn't about to be put off that easily, though. The things she needed to say had been rattling around inside her head for hours that night – and for a lot longer besides.

40

"It's not just the kids, either," she said into the darkness. "I miss you, too, believe it or not. You work so much lately… it's crazy."

It was an old argument, re-fought and replayed many times. Al was in no mood for another round. He made a noncommittal noise, pulled back the bedclothes and slid beneath the covers. "What can I do? They need me."

Lexi crossed to her side of the bed quickly, quietly, clicking on her bedside lamp and pulling the covers off of her side of the mattress with a flourish—theatrically, almost violently—partially uncovering Al, too, in a show of passive-aggression.

"Why?" she asked, letting the anger creep into her voice, not wanting to fight any more than Al did, but unable to help herself. She stood by the bed, staring at Al. He turned away, refusing to meet her gaze. "Why does it always have to be *you*, Al? Isn't there someone else? Can't you ever take a break? What about a vacation? We haven't gone anywhere since before Kyle was born. They have to give you some time to—"

Al rolled over, putting his back to her, closing his eyes, trying to close out the discussion in which he'd yet to participate. "Turn out the light and go to sleep, Lexi."

Lexi felt her eyes begin to sting; her whole face felt hot and a lump grew in her throat. The desperation she spent a great deal of time convincing herself she didn't feel washed over her. Her hand flew to her face as the tears began to seep from beneath her tightly closed eyelids.

"I can't keep raising these kids alone, Al. They're yours, too," she nearly whispered.

Back still turned, Al remained impassive. "Go to sleep, Lexi."

Lexi Vacarro bit her lip hard enough to hurt. She could taste blood as she climbed into the cold bed, excruciatingly aware of how wide a king-sized mattress could seem.

Two feet away, Al felt the vibrations of the sobs she tried to stifle, but convinced himself it was his imagination.

5

"If that's what you want, son, it's fine by me. In fact," Tony Vacarro smiled, "I'd be proud."

"Cool, pop." Sixteen-year-old Al Vacarro played casual, trying to hide the excitement he felt, trying to exude the nonchalant confidence his father always had. "I'll tell the school tomorrow, then."

"The hell you will!"

Father and son both turned towards Gina Vacarro, wife and mother of each, respectively. Her eyes blazed at the two men seated across the kitchen table from her. Against every instinct she had, she'd remained silent so far, hoping her husband would talk their boy out of this foolishness. She was aghast at what had happened instead.

"What are you thinking, Alfy? You wanna drop out of school with a year and a half left?" She stood, stomped across the short distance between them and cuffed the teenager across the back of his head, hard. "What's the matter with you?"

"Hey, Gina... relax." Tony's voice was calm, placating. "Don't hit the boy."

"Yeah, ma," Al added, rubbing his head gingerly. "Be cool. What do I want with school, anyway? I'm barely making grade as it is and it's not like I need any of that bulls — uh… crap."

"What about college?" Al's mother demanded. "What about getting a decent job?"

Al almost laughed at the prospect of college. Of more schooling. He could barely stand to sit through the basics. As if he'd subject himself to more of that junk. For what? To get some boring job he didn't want, anyway? He could read, he could write, he knew a little history and a little math. What the hell more did you need? But he knew what he didn't need - the trouble laughter would bring.

He raised an eyebrow, made a questioning expression. "Ma, weren't you listenin'? I'm gonna work with Pop. For Mister Castella."

Gina's face closed off. "I said a *job*. A career. What your father does isn't work, it's —"

"Gina," Tony's tone was no longer gentle, carrying instead a hint of something dark and dangerous. "It puts food on the table and a roof over our heads, don't it?"

He stood, placed one hand on her elbow and the other on her hip, gently guiding her back to her seat. "Mister Castella's been good to me — to us — for a long time. Let the kid help repay some of that good will, huh?"

Gina Vacarro remembered when the "arrangement" her husband had with the Castellas began - when it was supposed to be short-term, just to get them through a rough patch. Tony had been laid off from the moving company and hadn't been able to find more work, other than the occasional odds and ends that paid by the day and with no guarantee there would be work the next. And then there was the pregnancy scare on top of everything. Gina was sure she was pregnant and sure that it would ruin them, that their lives were over. They were in no position to raise a child. Money hadn't been tight, it'd been downright scarce.

But pregnancy or no, they still needed to eat, needed a place to live and for that, they needed an income. Gina never learned how Castella even became aware of Tony. They both had heard of him, but they weren't his type of people – they were beneath his notice. However it happened, the offer had been made and it terrified her. Gina begged Tony to turn it down, to say no in a way that wouldn't offend the man or his messenger. Tony, for the first time since she'd known him, had said "no," had put his foot down – to Gina, not Castella. Not only that, he worked hard at convincing her that it was the best they could hope for, that the offer from Castella's organization would get them back on their feet, ensure she and the baby they thought she was carrying would be provided for in the immediate future. And in the long-term, in exchange for helping with a few "jobs," Tony would be assured a real one – a straight job that both he and his soon-to-be family could be proud of. No argument she could think of was enough to even make him consider saying no to Castella's man. In the end, she relented only because it was clear that her options were to relent or lose the man she loved.

It was only after Tony had gone through with it, had sealed the deal and taken care of a couple of those nebulous "jobs" for Castella, that Gina's "little friend" had come back for a visit – nearly two months late. Stress, the doctor told her. It happened. It was nothing to worry about. But it *was* something to worry about – there were repercussions that worrying over money, over their situation, had wrought. If it hadn't been for that scare, that pregnancy that never was, would her husband have gone down the road he had? Would they be sitting at this table having this discussion? She had to wonder.

And even after living this life for nearly two decades, she still wondered. She'd learned to accept her husband's choices, had even learned to enjoy a measure of the prestige being married to one of Eddie Castella's top hands brought, but that was as far as it went. Bringing their child into it wasn't something she could forgive. Didn't Tony realize how precarious their lives were? He had been very lucky for a long time; she had met or heard of any number of other women whose husbands were part of Tony's "thing," as the men called it, who weren't as lucky. Not by half. And it was only a matter of time until that luck of

Tony's ran out. That wasn't anything Gina wanted for her only child. She'd agreed, so long ago, to let Tony have his way because it was that or lose him – and in a sense, she'd lost him anyway. Now he was asking her to let her son go down that very same road.

And what could she do? Al—her Alfy—was her baby boy. Her precious gift from God – the best part of the life she'd made so many mistakes in. And she did her best for him, trying to bring him up the way she herself was raised. She tried to instill in him respect and love and all the elements needed to become a decent human being. Things she'd once seen in Tony, things she only realized the true importance of when that thing of his began to crush them out of the man she'd fallen in love with, leaving in his place a familiar-looking stranger.

It was true that Tony Vacarro radiated charisma, a mixture of charm and power that people were drawn to. It wasn't hard to understand why. Tony was a winner in so many of the ways that the world said a man ought to be. But the things he'd done to gain what he had... even the thought made Gina shudder. And what did money and power matter against your eternal soul? It was a question Gina asked him once. It was the first time he'd ever hit her. It was a slap, openhanded, across the face. Just a smack to shut her up, he'd called it later, when he apologized for it. But it was enough to break something between them. And worse than that, Al was in the room when it happened. The look on the boy's face was something Gina Vacarro would never forget. Surprise and... something she couldn't place. Wonder, maybe. But tinged with fear – as if in that moment he learned something he'd thought to be undeniable truth was only an illusion.

Gina imagined it to be something like *"mom and dad aren't 'mom and dad',"* one unit, inseparable, as parents must appear to small children. Al learned that day that his parents were "mom" and "dad," two different, separate, entities, and moreover that "dad" was in charge.

It wasn't just Tony and Gina. Something changed between Gina and Al that day, too. He still loved her; there was no doubt about that. But he was never quite her little boy again. How he saw her was altered in a way that could never be repaired. And it had only gotten worse the older he got. She saw it in the way he looked at her even now. That mixture of pity and condescension in her son's eyes struck her in a way she couldn't ever really articulate. It wasn't right, she was sure of that much. It wasn't anything a mother should see when she looks at her child. But was he still hers? She was his mother, but it seemed all of a sudden that he'd been Tony's child for a long time. His and his alone.

She made a decision. She stood. "Do whatever you want. I don't want no part of it."

She disappeared through the kitchen doorway. A moment later, the apartment door opened then slammed shut.

Al and his father exchanged a look.

Tony shrugged. "She'll get over it."

***

Gina Vacarro didn't get over it.

As days turned to weeks and months, her son spent more time outside of the house, coming home only to sleep. And when Al was home, he became more tight-lipped, sharing looks, sharing secrets, with his father that she couldn't decipher, but still understood, as an insurmountable distance grew between her and the men who had once been her family. These two men, one the only man she'd ever loved, and the other born from her very body, became strangers.

The week before Al Vacarro's seventeenth birthday, a month after Christmas, the boy returned home from "work" late one snowy, blustery night to find a note taped to his bedroom door. It read:

Alfy,

I can't watch the same mistakes be made all over again. One time was too much. Despite it all, no matter what you think, I love you. I guess maybe too much. Be safe.

Love, always,

Your Mother, Gina

46

The teenager scoffed at the overly dramatic gesture, like something out of a TV movie-of-the-week. *She'll get over it*, his father said and Tony Vacarro had never lied to him, had never been wrong so far as he could see.

There was a first time for everything.

***

Al groaned in his sleep, rolled over. As he did, his outstretched hand brushed Lexi's back; still half-awake, she recoiled unconsciously.

***

The building was rundown—crumbling would be more accurate—but despite its dilapidation, it had probably once been a nice place to live. Even now, there were probably worse places, and the soft, fading light of early evening went a long way towards covering up many of its flaws.

"This is really it, pop?" Al turned his gaze from the building towards his father, already heading up the short steps of the concrete stoop.

"Sorry, kiddo, our regular room at the Ritz was booked. Get up here," Tony said, with a jerk of his head, his tone edging towards sharp.

Tony rarely had a cross word for his son, but Al had realized, even in the short time he'd been working with his father, that questioning anything about any part of the process would raise the other man's ire. As long as the older Vacarro had been doing this, it seemed he'd never fully gotten over the case of nerves each new day's potential risks brought. Al guessed it was why his father had lasted as long as he had, while many of the others he'd come up through the ranks with had been left by the wayside, in one fashion or another. He wanted to ask, but he never would. He was inexperienced, but not stupid.

Al couldn't blame his father for being cautious today, though – this meeting with elements of the Cotton Hill gang, who ran protection and other minor operations for Castella in certain areas of the city, was not off to the best start. The regular meeting spot—an under-the-table betting parlor Stewart Moretti, leader of the Cotton Hill crew, made his personal office—had been raided by cops earlier in the week. Castella's people were still looking into the hows, whys and whos of that particular fiasco. Enough cops were paid well and often enough that no raid should have taken them by surprise. In the meantime, this apartment-building, used as a sort of safe-house by Moretti, had been turned into temporary office quarters for the underboss. The location had only been provided to Castella's organization a couple of hours earlier, though, leaving no chance to check it out beforehand. That didn't sit well with anyone, least of all Tony Vacarro, whose lap this fiasco had been dropped into.

Al didn't understand why the meeting couldn't be called off, moved to another day, another place and time of Castella's choosing. Why there weren't more of them, at least. Tony was a big shot; surely Castella could spare more men for him than just his son and Ronnie Campagna, a boy less experienced even than Al, still in his first month on the job and only there at all because both Tony and Al had vouched for him.

Al had learned not to question his father, but the situation seemed extraordinary and he'd screwed up his courage and asked his father about all of these things. For once, Tony hadn't gotten angry at being questioned. Instead, he flat-out ignored Al and his concerns. That made Al more than a little uncomfortable, but what did he know? He'd been at this a few months shy of a year; Tony had almost twenty years' experience. The man must have known what he was doing, Al told himself.

Beyond those concerns, however, were more mundane ones: the Vacarros were late. Some sort of traffic snarl more than a dozen blocks away left them moving at a snail's pace, fuming all the while. Tony's anger was obvious, but at least he hadn't taken it out on the boys. Instead, he'd made an executive decision to leave Ronnie with the car until the boy could meet up with them, and walk the rest of the way.

Even with ten blocks still between them, they'd move faster on foot than by car, the way traffic was going.

"These things happen. They can't blame us, right?" Ronnie had asked, worry in his voice as the other two exited the vehicle. Tony hadn't even bothered replying.

Al took the six steps of the stoop two at a time and entered the building on his father's heels.

Inside, it was quiet, Al noted, in a way no apartment building he'd ever been in before was. It wasn't long til supper-time; people should be coming home from work, or wherever they spent their days, cooking meals, welcoming each other home, making a thousand different noises that they probably weren't even aware of just by being present. Even if this was a place where people mostly kept their heads down, there should have been *some* evidence that people were here.

From somewhere down a first-floor hallway, past the stairs leading higher into the building, Al heard a door creak open, followed by snatches of tinny, canned laughter, as from a TV show's laugh-track, and then a slam as, presumably, the same door closed again. He let out a breath, easing some of the tightness in his chest, and chided himself for his skittishness. Caution was one thing; being a pussy was another.

There was no elevator in the old building. The pair made their way up a switchback flight of stairs. The walls of the stairway were lightly dosed with graffiti—colorful renderings of names or just initials—and small pieces of litter, mostly cigarette butts and candy wrappers, had accumulated in the corners of the landings. They moved upwards past the second floor landing and on towards the third, the building's top floor. Down a long, narrow corridor dimly lit by a single bulb midway along its length, they passed neglected and ramshackle doors on either side of the hallway, years of wear and tear leaving no two looking alike save for similar combinations of numbers and letters: "3-A," "3-B," one simply marked "3-," where presumably a "C" had once been.

They stopped before a door marked "3-E," the last door on the right-hand side of the hallway, its surface more recently painted than the other doors', but still scuffed and stained with the passage of time and many people. Al wondered if anyone actually lived in this apartment or if it was solely used as the Cotton Hill crew's hidey-hole.

Tony threw a look at his son, checked the holster snugged beneath his left shoulder, concealed by the custom cut of his jacket, nodded and said, "I'll introduce you, vouch for you, but then you keep quiet. Let me do the talking. You just stay back, watch, listen... keep your head together and your eyes sharp."

"Sure thing, pop."

Tony nodded again then knocked on the door, calling softly, "Confed-Ex. Here for a package pickup."

A moment passed, then another.

Tony knocked again, harder this time. *Knock knock knock*!

"Anyone alive in there?"

Al grew nervous at the phrasing. It seemed poorly worded, and he suspected it somehow betrayed Tony's own fears. Al looked towards his father, whose eyes narrowed as his expression grew hard. The teenager opened his mouth, but Tony beat him to it: "Fuck it. Let's go. This is all wrong."

Relief washed over Al, but he was wise enough not to let it show. "Yeah, okay. If you think that's best."

They turned, heading back in the direction of the stairs, when a soft click behind them stopped both men's forward progress. Al looked over his shoulder as a tall, handsome man in his early middle years, wearing an off the rack charcoal-grey suit, stepped out of apartment 3-E's doorway, a small revolver in one hand and a walkie-talkie in the other.

"Only two of 'em. Converge on third. I've got positive ID on Anthony Vacarro, other is an unknown," he said into the radio as a pair of uniformed police officers crowded into the hall after him, squeezing past the man, headed towards the Vacarros.

"You there," the suited man said, pointing directly at Al with the weapon clutched in his fist. "Vacarro and friend. Police, stop right there. Put your hands up on the back of your head, fingers interlaced."

"Zimmerman? Shit!" Tony spat, years of self-taught training and hard-won experience apparently overtaking sense as his hand flew to his jacket and came out again in an instant, the gun blazing almost the moment it left the holster. Before Al's brain could even register *cop* or *men with guns*, one of the uniformed policemen staggered backwards against the wall of the narrow hallway and slid down towards the floor, his blood leaving a savage smear to mark his passage.

Tony turned on his heel, pushing Al before him, screaming, "Go! Go! Go!"

Al went, went, went, low and scrambling. His own weapon, tucked in the pocket of his brand-new suit-jacket, was forgotten as rounds flew overhead and a voice repeatedly demanded that he and his father stop where they were. Another voice, farther away, shouted, "Shots fired! Officer down!" and was met with a crackle-filled response from a radio. The words were muffled, but the electronic echo of the words seemed loud enough in the small, dingy corridor, to rival the firearms' reports.

The stairs were only feet away when something crashed into the wall next to Al's head. His eyes went wide, his ears rang as he turned, half-dazed, to see his father leaning against the dirty, paint-peeling plaster, one hand futilely trying to staunch the flow of blood streaming from his side, his teeth bared in a rictus of pain and rage.

"Get the fuck... outta here, Alfy," Tony hissed, not sparing his son a look as he fired wildly back towards the two, still standing, cops. "You ain't got a record and they don't know you. Keep it that way."

"Pop, but—"

"Go!" Tony roared over the voice of the guns.

Al turned, half-stumbling, half-running down the stairs, teeth sunk into the soft flesh inside his cheek in helpless frustration, tears filling the corners of his eyes – straight into the path of three more cops. They came up the switchback stairs, guns drawn, weighed down by heavy boots and thirty or more pounds of gear, but hurrying, racing to support their comrades.

"Fuck!" Al cried, eyes falling on his only option: the single window on the landing above where the cops had stopped.

The lead cop, a middle-aged black man with closely cropped hair and a salt-and-pepper mustache, caught Al's eye and apparently his train of thought. "Don't do it, son."

Al grit his teeth, backed up a few steps, then pushed off with one foot like a sprinter and ran full-tilt towards the window.

***

"It's a God-damned tragedy is what it is."

Eddie Castella blew a smoky sigh up towards the ceiling fan whirling lazily overhead, apparently fascinated for a moment by the interplay of moving air and smoke. He took another heavy drag off of his cigarette, its glowing tip flaring to devour the last half inch of the thing. He held it a moment, then released the breath sharply and stubbed the cigarette out in the ashtray before him.

Al sat across from Castella, the big, dark wood desk in Eddie's tiny office between them, feeling more like a wall than a workspace, bisecting the small room as it did. Al said nothing, staring at an imaginary point on the wall beyond Castella. The bandages on Al's arms, cut to shit when he'd jumped through that window, itched like hell; the scrapes on his face glowed a dull, angry red that matched his mood. The escape from the raid, trap, whatever it was, still didn't seem real. It was nothing more than a jumble of confused images and half-memories of fleeing down alleys, ducking into buildings and running, running, running until he was sure that his lungs would explode and his legs would buckle. He still wasn't sure how he'd managed.

No, that wasn't right. When he tried to remember, it was nothing but a blank, but suddenly a sequence came back to him, as clearly as if he was watching it on a movie screen.

He'd crashed through the window, landed in a bleeding heap in the alley, somehow managing to scramble to his feet and run. He wasn't familiar with the neighborhood, but no direction meant anything more than any other, so as long it took him away from the crumbling tenement where his father had intended to meet with the Cotton Hill crew.

So he'd run, flat-out, for three blocks or so then turned down an alley, only to discover it was a dead-end, blocked by a ten-foot tall brick wall, seemingly randomly placed in the middle of the alley. Sirens growing louder behind him, he'd cursed and swore and hauled himself up onto the wall by sheer force of will. He'd been about to simply leap down the other side and keep running when inspiration struck and, instead, he leapt onto the fire escape of one of the buildings, only a couple of feet higher than the wall. He'd scrambled up it, praying nobody in any of the apartments saw him, heard the sirens and put two and two together— or if they did, were the kind of people who minded their own damned business, rather than dial 911—and onto the roof where he'd continued running, leaping the three feet from that building to the next. He'd repeated the process twice more before finding a rooftop with an open door leading into the building itself, then scrambled down into its interior, all the way down into its basement before exiting through a service entrance and continuing to run until he could no longer hear sirens in the distance. Whatever luck had abandoned Tony Vacarro had fled to Al, it seemed.

He tried not to think of it or of the pain, either the physical kind that suffused his body or the kind clawing away at the depths of his brain. Tried not to think about the pain, even while he was sure that it would dog him for a long, long time to come. Instead, he focused on keeping his face an impassive mask as he waited for Castella to continue whatever train of thought he'd begun.

At last: "Hey, kid," the older gangster said softly. "What do *you* think?"

"Yeah, Mister Castella..." Al wasn't sure what the right answer was. Of course it was a God-damned tragedy, but obviously that wasn't what Eddie wanted to hear. Why tell the man what he already knew?

"But, uh—" Al looked up, met the other man's gaze.

"But that ain't all," Castella finished for him. "It was a set-up. A tragedy someone, you know… *engineered*, I guess is the word." Castella's tone turned icy.

Al's mouth worked silently for a moment, his brain gnawing on the statement, trying to fit this piece into the puzzle of the last few hours. Finally: "Wh-what do you mean?" But he knew. The second he said it, the answer came to him.

"Al, my boy," Castella's tone turned paternal, "We got ourselves a fuckin' *leak*. A *rat*."

"Shit." The single word confirmed what he'd already been thinking, what he hadn't wanted to allow himself to believe.

It was too coincidental; the Cotton Hill crew lose their headquarters then want to talk strategy with the *capo* about straightening things, reorganizing – all that made sense. But the unusual meeting place, the lack of any real notice, and the cops waiting for Tony at the "safe-house"… It was so obviously a set-up that it hurt Al to think his dad had walked into it. Tony seemed to know something, too… he'd called out that cop's name, hadn't he? What the fuck did *that* mean? And *why*? What the fuck had happened and had it really only been a couple of hours ago? It seemed to Al like it happened to a different person, like Al Vacarro had gone into that building but someone else had come out.

"Son of a bitch," Al swore, barely more than a whisper.

"You got that right, Al, my man." Castella face was stone as he added, "And I know just the one."

***

With a supreme act of will, Ronnie Campagna broke his gaze from the barrel of the snub-nosed revolver and turned red, swollen eyes on Al. If looks could kill, Ronnie would be dead already; he almost preferred staring down the gun.

"I, I don't understand, Al!" he said for the hundredth time. "C'mon, I get what happened's fucked and your head is probably messed up right now, but if I pissed you off somehow, lemme make it up to you!"

It'd been half an hour, at least, and Al still hadn't said a word. At least Al had stopped hitting him. A trickle of blood still ran from Ronnie's temple, skirting the lid of his left eye to mix with the tears of fear and pain that were slowly drying on his cheeks.

"We're friends, ain't we? We've *always* been friends, right? You don't treat friends like—"

"Like what, Ronnie?" Al cut in, breaking his silence at last. "Like stepping stones? Like get out of jail free cards, Ronnie?"

Ronnie shook his head slowly, wary of the weapon and Al's state of mind. Softly, he said, "I don't know what you mean."

"Fuck you, you don't." Al pressed the tip of the weapon into Ronnie's forehead, hard enough to bruise. *Not that it would matter*, Al thought.

The tears began to well up again. Ronnie couldn't help it. "Whatever you're thinking," he choked out, "it's not like that."

"Why did you do it?" Al's voice was almost gentle. "C'mon, tell me. Did you want out already? Did they make you some sort of deal? They must have. You ain't even been in a month yet, have you? You haven't done shit, so what could you possibly know? And then this thing with Moretti fell right into your lap. Or maybe this was the plan from the very start? Was Moretti part of it, too? He must have been. Both of you must'a been at this from the get-go. Shit." Al was rambling and he was aware of it. He took a huge, gulping breath, like the air in the room was suddenly too thin, like he was struggling to get oxygen to his brain.

His gaze bored into his friend as he said, "Ronnie, you never showed no interest in any of this, did you? Then all of a sudden, you ask if there's work for you. I should'a been suspicious, I guess, but you were my friend, so I never even questioned it. Who's gonna be scared of Ronnie the Mouse, huh?" He tried to force a laugh, but it turned into a strangled sort of choking sound.

Al cleared his throat then squatted on his haunches, bringing his face level with Ronnie's. "Did someone come up to you one day and say, 'Listen, we know who your friends are'? Something like that? Some

55

cop or lawyer, offering you what – money?" Al shook his head slowly, eyes closed.

Ronnie was glad for the reprieve from that terrible gaze, even if it was only momentary.

When they opened again, Al's eyes were distant, no longer focused on Ronnie, but on some point beyond him. "It don't matter, though, I guess." He stood. He sighed. "Fuck, Ronnie... my *dad*. He was good to you. He was good to all of us."

"I didn't do *shit!*" Ronnie screamed, his voice echoing shrilly through the cavernous warehouse to which Al had brought him – some shipping business owned by the Castellas. It must be after three a.m. by now, Ronnie guessed. It didn't matter how loud he was, so why not let it out? The ache in his gut—from the beating and the berating, both— told him there was nothing to lose.

"I didn't do anything, Al. The fuckin' traffic, the pile-up or whatever it was—"

"Cut it out, Ronnie. Be a fuckin' man."

Ronnie took a deep, shuddering breath. "Al, I swear on my ma's life—"

"Don't you dare. You already killed my pop. You wanna get your mom killed, too?"

Ronnie's jaw clenched so hard, his back teeth started creaking. The self-inflicted pain was almost welcome; somehow, it kept his mind off of the throbbing in the rest of his body, letting him focus on the anger that was slowly overtaking the fear that had filled him.

"I wanna know who says it's me," he said quietly, looking up through blood and tear-crusted lashes at Al. Ronnie was always small, but the angle and the effect made him look very young, even to Al's eyes.

"I'm owed that much at least, aren't I, Al? I wanna name so I know who to curse when I'm down in hell."

Al almost laughed. Almost. The show of bravado was laughable. Too little, too late. Where were Ronnie's guts the whole rest of his damned life? And why would he use them to betray people who'd been nothing but friends to him? It didn't make any sense, none of this made any sense, but fuck, his dad was dead. That much he understood. That he knew to be fact. Killed at the scene, the report from Castella's pet cops said. Castella already heard by the time Al made it back to the *capo*'s place and he hadn't been idle in the hours between hearing of it and telling Al.

"Eddie," Al answered, almost offhandedly, forcing casualness into his tone. "Eddie himself says he's got good info it was you, Ronnie. Not just information, *proof*. Now you see why I'm so sure?"

"No, I don't, Al. Cuz you known me your whole life. Eddie? So what? Who the fuck is he to you? He's a bigshot, but he ain't your *friend*, is he? I am. I always have been. You already made up your mind, but I'll swear to you on anything you want me to, *I didn't do this thing* and whatever proof Eddie says he's got, it's made up. It's a God-damned lie!"

"Why did you even want in on our thing, Ronnie?" It was said so calmly, so naturally, as if the conversation couldn't have led anywhere else, that it took Ronnie aback for a moment. "You say it wasn't a set-up, you weren't workin' for anybody in trying to get in, but you never showed no interest in it before. Then out of nowhere... you want in. And then this whole fucked up mess of a night happens. It's suspicious, ain't it? You see what I mean, right?"

Ronnie swallowed, blinked away the wateriness in his eyes, buying seconds to think. From Al's perspective, yeah, he could see how it was suspicious – if it was anyone else. Not Ronnie. Ronnie the Mouse, the name Mike had stuck him with years ago. Ronnie who never hurt a fly.

I'm your fuckin' friend! he wanted to scream again, as if it answered all of Al's questions, as if they were magic words that would wipe away all traces of doubt. But he'd tried that – had been trying it for who could say how long now. An hour? Two? Shit, it didn't matter. And he didn't have any answers to Al's questions. Not one the other boy would accept.

"I don't know," he said at last. "Cuz everyone was doin' it, I guess."

"Yeah, I thought so. Shitty reason. No God-damned reason at all, really." Al sighed, took a step back, lowered the gun – but not enough so Ronnie wasn't still covered. "You know why me and Mikey and most of the other guys do this?"

Ronnie waited. When Al said nothing else, apparently wanting an actual answer from him, he shook his head slowly.

"Because," Al continued. "It's in our *blood*. You grew up with us, Ronnie, but you were never like us. You were never gonna be cut out for this life."

It was true, Ronnie realized. He'd always realized that, on some level, as close as he and Al and Mike had been as kids, he wasn't like them. And it was never more apparent than the instant he first set foot in the Castellas' stronghold. Something had grabbed at his balls, something that felt like fear and panic and hurt all wrapped up in one painful instant. An instant when every fiber of his being screamed at him to run away – like it was now.

"I know," Ronnie said. "I'm a no-good pussy and I'm not cut out for this, like you said. But I didn't have anything to do with your pop gettin' snapped, Al, so if you kill me, you're doin' it for Castella. Just cuz he said so, and not for your dad."

"Prove it."

"How can I?" Ronnie snarled through still-clenched teeth, suddenly furious at the ridiculous request.

"'S'not my problem to figure out," Al said with cruel indifference. "You make a statement like that, you're the one's gotta back it up."

Ronnie looked down at the cold cement he'd been kneeling on for so long that he'd lost all sensation in his legs. Dark wet spots appeared on the floor, within the outline his shadow, cast by the harsh florescent lighting, high above their heads. He fell forward onto his hands and knees. "Al... *please* don't do this." He choked, the words sticking his throat. "Please, Al. I'm your friend. I've *always* been your friend."

"But you aren't family," Al said, simply, as he pulled the trigger, filling the huge, empty building with an instant of cacophony.

***

Revenge wasn't sweet. If Al was honest, killing Ronnie Campagna somehow made it feel like his dad had died all over again.

On the drive back to Castella's place, to tell the big man that the job was done and to make arrangements for clean-up, Al tried to keep his mind blank, to focus on the mechanical motions of driving. On the road in front of him. On the curves and lines and shapes of the street-signs and lamp-posts. On the pressure of his foot against the gas pedal, of the smooth leather covering the wheel grasped in his hands. Anything to keep from thinking about what he had done and about what had been said.

But the thought appeared unbidden: *Ronnie knew he was going to die, knew Castella had proof he was the rat... so not come out and admit it?*

What was the point, Al wondered. A few more minutes, hours, days... maybe weeks, at best, of life? Did he even believe that was possible? It seemed unlikely.

It was even more unlikely, but... was it possible Ronnie was telling the truth?

Was Castella? Why *wouldn't* he? What purpose would throwing Ronnie into the maw of the monster that Al's vengeance had briefly become serve if he wasn't the one who'd done this horrible thing?

Al wondered. And he always would.

***

Al awoke with a start, his mouth gummy and foul-tasting, his throat full of phlegm. He rolled over, looked at the bedside clock: the display showed 3:34 a.m., glowing blood-red in the darkness.

Almost the exact same time, Al thought.

The black stillness of the room was broken by a snort and a small grunt as Lexi, too, turned over, the rhythm of her breathing interrupted. Al lay motionless, not wanting to further disturb her. Half a moment passed before the soft snoring resumed.

Slowly, carefully, Al leaned over. His eyes adjusted to the almost total darkness, he could just make out the outlines of Lexi's features. He brushed the hair away from her face and kissed her lightly on the brow. "I'm sorry, baby," he whispered. "Every damned time, I'm sorry."

He slid off of the bed, padded across the room and out into the hallway, faintly lit by a single, low-wattage nightlight at the far end, down by the kids' rooms. He went into the bathroom, lit by a small light, twin to the one in the hallway, plugged into a socket over the sink and relieved himself, forgoing flushing or washing his hands, not wanting to risk the noise. By the gloomy light of the tiny night-lamp, he glanced at himself in the bathroom mirror, hating what he saw: the thinning hair, the lines around his eyes, the man who looked back at him through those eyes.

He exited the bathroom, wandering down the hallway back towards the bedroom. He was at the entryway when something made him turn his head. He saw light coming from beneath Beth's door. He approached quietly, opened the door a crack, slowly to avoid its hinges' tendency to creak. The girl lay on top of the bedclothes, arms and legs akimbo, the book she'd been reading when Al first came home fallen open on her thin chest, rising and falling with her breath.

He smiled despite her defiance. Getting back up to read again, after he'd explicitly told her to get to sleep, was Beth in a nutshell. Al tiptoed into the room, clicked off the table-lamp then quickly exited again, closing the door behind him. "That girl, I swear," he mumbled, but the smile remained in place.

On a whim, he opened Kyle's door, too. He peeked in on the boy who still slept soundly, as he had earlier, peaceful in whatever place his dreams conjured. For an instant, Al felt a pang of envy, a longing for the blissful ignorance in which the little boy lived – unaware of anything more than his tiny world of home, family, school and friends. Unaware of the darkness that lay just outside those small circles. The darkness his father lived in.

Al couldn't remember what that ignorance was like, wasn't sure he'd ever even *had* that. Even as a relatively small child, he'd had an inkling of what his father's — now his — world was like, even if he didn't have the particulars until he was much older.

Wonder if the old man ever watched me sleep. The thought popped into Al's mind, fully formed and instantly painful.

He grimaced, pursing his lips in quiet disgust at such foolishness. He backed slowly, silently, out of the room.

"Why do I fuckin' do this to myself?" he asked of no one in particular. "I need a drink."

He headed down the stairs, thinking of the bottles in the cabinet over the refrigerator, to pass the hours until the start of the coming day.

6

The sun shone down on a day that promised heat, but had not yet made good on its intentions. Al was glad. He didn't do well with heat. The suit and tie didn't help, but he was old-school. Respectable blandness was the best cover. Nobody looked twice at a middle-aged man in a half-decent suit and a department store tie. Let the schlubs and wannabes wander around in their tracksuits and gold chains, looking like slobs, standing out like a Hollywood stereotype and catching attention everywhere they went.

Al's gaze wandered towards the passenger seat of the Crown Vic. Benny may have been a violent idiot, but at least he dressed in dignified fashion.

It was still morning, though only by the barest margin. Rush hour was long over, and the streets were mostly empty, save for a few passersby here and there — women and old men, mostly — going about their business, many in the leisurely way of people who had nowhere to be on a weekday morning. It was a neighborhood where people either worked themselves to the bone or didn't work at all – the sort of low-income, working-class community you could find anywhere in the world. A place you were either born to or fell in to, but regardless of how you got there, once you had, you simply *belonged* because there was nowhere else for you to be.

Of course there were exceptions. Neither Al nor Benny belonged there, but it was still exactly where they were supposed to be. And though they appeared in no hurry — Al, sitting behind the wheel of the car, sipped coffee and browsed the day's paper; Benny next to him, scanned the streets ahead of them, flicking a lighter on and off listlessly, mechanically — their day's work had already begun.

Al glanced back down at the sports page folded open on his lap, but it was pointless; his concentration was lost. His eyes drifted back towards Benny, down to the lighter the younger man toyed with, to the flame that burst into life and disappeared as quickly. The sight of the tiny, dancing flame flicking in and out of existence had a hypnotic quality, but the sound drove Al nuts. He winced at every rasping *click, flick, click, flick* sequence of noises the lighter made.

Annoying little fuck, Al thought, tearing his eyes away. He had to admit, though, that annoying as it was, the sound was still better than Benny talking.

"Would you look at this asshole?" Benny said, as if on cue.

Al sighed and followed Benny's gaze toward the nearby intersection, through which a sun-faded, yellow- and black-checkered cab slowly rolled. A middle-aged guy who looked Indian or Middle Eastern sat behind the wheel, a large plastic travel-mug to his lips and one eye plastered to a newspaper propped before him on the steering wheel. In the backseat of the vehicle, a young woman chattered animatedly into a cellphone, lips flapping and gesturing frequently with her free hand.

"He's drinkin' a coffee and readin' the paper. So what? Me, too."

"You ain't drivin', Al." Benny's tone was aghast. "Professional like that oughta know better."

"Fair point." Al made a little facial shrug, not caring enough to put his shoulders into it. "But what the fuck do you care? It don't hurt you any," he added, drawn, despite himself, into this dumbass conversation.

Funny thing, though: he was actually glad Benny had brought it up, glad to find out something like that annoyed the kid. It was nice to hear that Benny thought about this stuff, nice to know he was something more than just a murderous poon-hound. Not much more, maybe, but it was a start. It gave Al something to consider, anyway.

"It's friggin' *dangerous*." Benny sounded exasperated. His thumb began flicking the lighter's flint-covered striker faster, the flame rapidly appearing and vanishing in that strangely mesmeric fashion.

Al shifted his gaze away from the dancing flame, blinking hard to rid himself of the red and orange afterimage burned into his retina. "So is playing with that damned lighter. Put it away before I take it away. I don't want you accidentally scorchin' up my upholstery."

"Whatever," Benny sulked, but the lighter disappeared into a pocket of his jacket – a white sport coat nearly identical to the one he'd worn the previous night, worn over a black turtleneck. This coat's cuffs were thankfully free of blood spatter. As Al watched, Benny's jaw began to clench, unclench, clench again as if he was chewing something he found hard to swallow. Al wondered, suddenly, what Benny thought about when he was alone.

Al turned his eyes back to the newspaper in his hands, but he no longer had even a passing interest in anything it said. He was a reluctant reader at best and the interruption, the conversation, had taken him out of the moment. He already heard the scores he cared about on the radio during his morning routine of shit, shower, shave. The paper was window-dressing. Two guys sitting in a parked car in the middle of the day was suspicious enough. It couldn't be helped, but at least one of them doing something mundane might take the edge off the red flags they were sending up.

Benny stared sullenly out of the open passenger window, his only distractions disappeared or forbidden. Al was reaching for the radio when Benny spoke again. "So these guys gonna show or what?"

Al glanced at the dashboard clock: 11:07 a.m. He took a long sip from his Styrofoam cup of now-cold coffee, draining it down to the dregs, frowning at the clumps of grounds stuck to the bottom, thinking

How hard is it to pour a cup of coffee? Out loud, he said, "Probably ain't even out of bed yet. 'Bangers are lazy motherfuckers."

Al opened the car door, leaned out, tossed the empty cup towards a garbage can sitting on the curb, next to and slightly behind the parked car. He watched with satisfaction as the refuse sailed cleanly into the receptacle. *Nothin' but net,* he thought, allowing himself a small, satisfied grin at the meaningless victory. It died when he caught sight of the pair coming around the corner.

Al ducked back into the car, pulling the door inwards, but not allowing it to latch. He sat ramrod straight in the seat and stared up into the rearview mirror.

The significance of his actions wasn't lost on Benny. "What?" he asked plainly.

"It's them." Al loosened the buttons on his jacket, freeing up access to the holster riding beneath his left shoulder. "The bag boys from Rojas Killas. They're comin' up the sidewalk behind us."

"What?" Benny drew the word out to three syllables in exaggerated surprise. "Well, shit. What happened to them comin' from Cork Street? That's where their crib is, right?"

Al shook his head almost imperceptibly, annoyed at the inanity of what Benny chose to focus on. He drew the nine-millimeter Browning pistol from its hiding place. "Who knows? Who *cares*?"

"Yeah, guess you're right." Benny admitted, pulling from his own jacket a big, Dirty Harry-style forty-four caliber Magnum revolver. It was less a firearm than it was a cannon. A lot of flashy overkill. It fit Benny perfectly. He grinned at the thing, a gleeful expression that replaced the bored one he'd been wearing all morning.

Without looking at the other man, Benny asked, "You want me to get this?" just as the pair in question sauntered past the parked car, totally unaware they were the subject of the other two men's discussion, their confident stride speaking of the conviction that they were the most dangerous denizens of this block.

"Nah." Al waved a hand distractedly towards Benny as he opened the car door again. "You got the last one. I'll handle it."

There was no one in sight but the two 'bangers. The timing would never be better.

Al stepped out of the vehicle, leaving the door open behind him – for a quick getaway or cover, if necessary. The car was halfway down the block; the Rojas Killas were nearly at the opposite corner, but still no more than a hundred feet away. He silently thanked whatever urban planners had decided on short blocks in this section of the city.

Al called out, "Hey, fellas," adding, "Yeah, you. The shit-heels with the pants that don't fit right."

As one, the two men turned. Al sized them up in an instant:

The nearer of them was a man younger than Benny, with a café au lait complexion that spoke of a mixed-race heritage and wild hair worn in a short sort of Afro. "The fuck you say, white-bread?" he spat, raising a dirt-'stache-covered lip in a sneer that mixed confusion and anger. He'd probably practiced it in the mirror, trying to look hard. Instead, it made his somewhat pudgy baby-face seem more ridiculous than threatening. Al decided he looked like an uncomfortably gassy infant.

Al ignored him, focusing on the other gangbanger, the one who presented real danger. This one was probably only slightly older than his comrade – though it was hard to get a solid read with the other one's baby-face – but something in the fine, dark-complexioned features struck Al as far more mature, more worldly – and more dangerous. Even at a distance, there was something inside those eyes that Al, killer that he was in his own right, found unsettling. This one wasted no words on confused bravado, he simply reached into the front pocket of his hooded sweatshirt for the weapon that bulged there.

The handsome kid with the killer eyes raised his weapon as Al dropped him, finger caressing the trigger of the Browning without conscious thought. A single round flashed from the barrel of the gun to bury itself in the other man's chest, directly beneath his right clavicle. The kid grunted, as if Al had done nothing more than slug him in the shoulder with his fist, struggled for half a moment to maintain his balance against the overwhelming force of the bullet then went down flat on his back onto the cracked, uneven sidewalk, his light grey hoodie turning a dark red. The sound of the gunshot hadn't finished bouncing off of the walls of the urban canyon around them before his struggles ceased.

The other gangbanger's eyes went wide. "Son of a bitch!" he screamed, drawing his weapon from the waistband of his oversized pants, recovering from his shock admirably – faster than Al expected of an amateur.

Not that it mattered. He dropped as quickly as his friend had, Al's second shot plowing straight through the kid's belly, sending him falling to the ground, somehow both screaming and gasping for breath.

Al stalked forward, eyes locked on the flopping, struggling form of the young man, who shrieked and thrashed, a look on his face as if he was unable to comprehend what had happened. He looked down at himself, eyes rolling wildly, still howling in pain, but somehow finding the presence of mind to press hands to his stomach in a futile attempt at holding his life's blood in.

Al saw all of that and put it aside, sparing a moment for the other gang-member, the one he'd first shot. It was clear that the kid was already dead, but Al had long ago decided on caution and thoroughness. He put a second bullet between the kid's eyes.

"Please, man," the still-living, gut-shot 'banger croaked through bloodied lips, looking even younger now than he had before. His cheeks were already growing pale, though whether from fear, shock or blood-loss was unclear. He reached upwards, one hand thrust out towards his attacker as if the other man would somehow, miraculously, have a change of heart and spare him from the same fate as his friend. He coughed, bloody sputum flying from between his lips, adding, "I got a kid…" as if it made a difference. Al squeezed the Browning's trigger a fourth time, making a hole in the boy's head that matched the one in his partner's.

Al walked quickly, but calmly, back towards the waiting car without another glance at the two men he'd killed. He slid behind the wheel, slammed the door and cranked the engine to life. "Let's get outta here."

"That was *amazin'*, man!" Benny grinned, elated, delighted with the spectacle. "You fuckin' wasted those pieces of shit like it was *nothin'*! They didn't even get a chance to draw down!"

Al hocked and spit out of the open window, as if trying to dislodge an unpleasant taste from his mouth. The vehicle pulled away from the curb smoothly, roaring towards and then around the same corner that the cab had earlier disappeared behind.

"It *was* nothin'. They were amateurs," Al said. "One of 'em was just a kid." *Both of 'em, probably*, he added to himself. "Not that big an accomplishment."

"Seriously?" Benny scoffed, disappointed at this dismissal of his sincerest praise. "Well," he added, "maybe now their boss'll finally take the hint, at least."

"Hope so," Al said, eyes glued to the street, slowing down as he approached a busy intersection where the 'hood began to taper out and slightly more upscale housing started to appear. "Kinda doubt it, though. That was the second time this month Castella's taken out Rojas soldiers." Quietly, he added, "'Least these two were older'n the last ones."

Benny looked at him askance. "You developin' a soft spot for this street trash, Al?"

The older man shook his head, just once, keeping his eyes on the road. "'Course not. Don't be stupid. Just a shame to waste such short lives."

Benny startled cackling, the sound loud and raucous in the confines of the car, startling Al with this unexpected reaction.

"Fuck's wrong with you?" His head twitched in Benny's direction, then back to the traffic ahead of him.

Wiping something from his eye, his laughter petering out into a low chuckle, Benny answered, "Nothin'. But it's funny, what you said. I mean, c'mon, their lives were wasted the second their boss crossed Castella, right?"

"Yeah… guess you're right," Al said, glumness creeping into his voice.

7

The bell over the door jingled as Al entered Manny's, Benny on his heels like a faithful, if slightly rabid, puppy. The heavy air of the diner, stirred by their entrance, swirled around them, carrying strains of conversation, kitchen noise and the mouthwatering smells of grease and coffee. The place wasn't large, but it also wasn't very busy. Even now, at lunch-time, only a few of the stools by the lunch-counter were occupied, and only a pair of the eight booths, evenly divided along either wall on opposite sides of the restaurant, held customers. None of these few customers paid the newcomers even momentary notice.

A brunette waitress, mid-thirties, heavy-set, but still sort of trashy-sexy, dressed in a too-tight pink and white uniform, approached, waving a pair of menus like a flag of surrender. "Seat yourselves anywhere, guys, I'll be along in a minute." She shoved the laminated sheets into Al's hand then retreated back behind the counter, putting the barrier between her and her patrons.

Al muttered, "Thanks," not caring that the woman wouldn't hear it, and headed towards the rearmost booth in the place, the one farthest from the entrance, that Martin Teehan favored, motioning for Benny to follow. The man himself was nowhere in sight, but Frankie and Jude, the nearly twin muscle-heads who served as Teehan's bodyguards, were seated at the counter nearby. Frankie nodded at Al respectfully as he passed, ignoring Benny. Jude ignored them both, engrossed in a wrestling magazine, his lips moving as he read.

Al and Benny sat on opposite sides of the thinly padded, red, faux-leather booth. Before they were even settled, Marty appeared from a short hallway off to the left, zipping his fly.

"Mornin', fellas. Hey, kid," this was directed towards Benny, along with a single, waggling finger. Benny looked blankly at the older man.

"Benny," Al said, scooting further into the booth. "Over here."

"Yeah, sure." Strangely compliant for once, Benny slid out of the booth and then back in again on Al's side, allowing Marty to squeeze his bulk into the other side of the table, giving him the whole bench to himself.

Castella's top lieutenant arranged his features into the facial crease that passed for a smile. His professional smile, at least. If he had any other, Al wasn't sure he'd ever seen it. Possibly once or twice when he was a kid, when Tony was still around. The two men had been good friends.

"You guys eat? Go ahead and order somethin'. They do breakfast all day here."

Benny picked up the single-page menu, began to browse the plastic-covered page, front and back. "They do those fancy waffles here? Got the fruit and whipped cream and shit?"

Al and Marty ignored him.

Marty asked, "So you guys have any trouble?"

Al shrugged one shoulder, a menu in his hand but his eyes on Marty's. "Nah, no real trouble. They came from Elm instead of Cork Street like we were expecting, but I made it work. They weren't carryin' anythin' that I could see, so they were probably just startin' for the day."

Marty's head bobbed and his mouth opened, but before he could respond, the waitress appeared at his elbow. "Ready to order, boys?'

"You don't got those waffles, the big fluffy ones?" Benny asked.

"Belgian? Nah. We got regular waffles, French toast or pancakes, hon'."

Al rolled his eyes. Marty's lips pressed into a hard line.

"Pancakes then, I guess. And some orange juice." Benny's disappointment was clear.

The woman turned towards Al. Seen close up and straight on, Al decided she'd be very pretty if she scraped off a layer or two of makeup. "And for you, sweetie?"

"Coffee and toast, butter on the side."

"All righty, be out in a few." The woman turned on her heels, wide hips swaying and plump bottom rolling beneath the straining fabric, without even a glance at Marty. Al wondered if the man had become such a fixture in the place she no longer even noticed him. This wasn't his only "open meet" spot, but Al had certainly met him here enough times over the years for the both of them to be considered regulars by the staff. He didn't like it, but it wasn't his decision. Like everything else, these days, all he could do was accept it.

Marty threw a look over his shoulder, watching the woman's retreating rear or making sure she was out of earshot—could be both— then opened his mouth to resume whatever he was going to say before being interrupted.

Benny beat him to the punch. "So you hear from that spic, what's his name, yet? The Rojas Killas boss? He's gotta know he's in the shit now, right?"

Marty threw Al a meaningful look. Al clenched his fist beneath the table and thought *The fuck am I supposed to do?*

Benny stared across the table at Marty, his eyes wide, unblinking, waiting like a curious kid that doesn't realize what he's even asked. Exactly what he was, Al decided.

Marty let out a tiny sound that could have been a sigh or a groan, but chose to answer. "Guzman. And no." He gestured with a single finger. "One, he probably ain't heard about it yet – it's been, what? Less than an hour? And two," he continued, raising another digit, "he either doesn't seem to give a shit we're takin' his hustlers out or he's got so many, we aren't even making a dent in his operation."

His eyes flicked from Benny to Al, who nodded agreement, saying, "Could go either way with these 'banger shitheads. They got no loyalty and most of 'em got no head for strategy. 'S'all about numbers with them. All they got to do is keep puttin' bodies on the street." He winced internally, instantly regretting his choice of words.

Marty picked up the thread. "Yeah, Al's right. It doesn't matter what these boys cost if Guzman never has to pay 'em, so he can put as many out there as he can scrounge up. Annoying, but what are you gonna do?" He slumped back against the seat. "Either way, it's only a matter of time. We'll show this motherfucker that it's all well and good if he wants to change suppliers – he just won't make any money until he changes *back* to Castella."

Al shifted in his seat, careful to hide his distaste. The killing didn't bother him, it was the *why*. As far as he was concerned, the 'bangers could have the drug trade. That shit just didn't sit well with Al and, until recently, even Castella wanted nothing to do with it. Girls, gambling, protection and loan rackets; those were time-honored, relatively honest ways to make money. They were services people wanted; somebody was going to provide them and it might as well be Castella.

That other stuff, though? Heroin, cocaine, crack and whatever the fuck else – it was filthy. Nothing but poison, turning people into the living dead, desperate, thinking of nothing but the next fix until they fell down dead for real. A bullet in the head Al had no problem with, if someone had earned it, but that other kind of death was nothing he wanted to be responsible for. Nobody deserved that and when Castella had announced that the organization was expanding into that trade, Al had argued against it. Argued and debated until he realized it wasn't safe to keep trying. The look in Castella's eye had told him where one more word would get him. The Castella Al knew as a young man didn't have any such look; he'd been dangerous if pushed, but he'd always been willing to listen to his friends and associates. The man he'd become the last few years, though, was a bitter stranger, without friends or confidantes, with Martin Teehan the only possible exception.

As if sensing the perfect lull in the conversation, the waitress reappeared, breakfast-laden tray in hand. She swiftly set down Benny and Al's food, filled Al's coffee mug and refreshed Marty's without being asked, said, "Enjoy, guys," then disappeared again through the nearby kitchen door.

Benny drowned his meal in syrup from a plastic carafe, then began shoveling huge chunks of sugar-soaked pancake into his mouth, making little noises of contentment. "Damn, this's good," he mumbled through a mouthful.

"Relax, Benny. Slow down. Nobody's gonna take it away from you." Al gave the kid a look of distaste, as he added two packets of sugar and a splash of creamer to his coffee. He stirred, took a sip. *Jesus, this kid even eats like an animal.*

"Glad you're enjoying it, Benny." Teehan seemed vaguely amused, the beginnings of a smile tugging at the corner of his lip before disappearing again. It was something of a minor miracle. The big Irish mobster wasn't known for his sense of humor. Al tried to remember ever hearing Teehan laugh.

Benny chewed, swallowed, forked in and chewed some more as Al and Marty drank coffee, each man keeping his thoughts to himself for the moment.

Pancakes gone, the associated noises ceased and a couple of minutes passed in silence. Benny's plate was empty, but Al's was still untouched, the toast gone cold. Benny eyed the food, wondering if Al would mind if he snagged it. Instead, he asked of no one in specific, "So what do we do now?"

"We wait," Al answered, then looked toward Marty for confirmation. "Right?"

Marty set his coffee cup down, the thick, commercial-grade dishware seeming fragile in his big, scarred hands. "Yeah. Mister Castella does, anyway. You got more work to do this afternoon."

Al bit his cheek to keep himself from wincing. "Magini, right?"

Marty's eyes met Al's. "You been lettin' him slide an awful lot, Al. Castella's not happy about that. He still checks the books himself, and he's still got a head for numbers."

"I know, but..." Al's head twitched in what might have been a tiny shake of the head. "Shit, he's an old man."

Benny looked from one man to the other, slightly confused, lost in the slim thread of the conversation. "You mean the drugstore guy, yeah? So what if he's an old man? He owes Mister Castella money, right? Like that Brentano dude. 'S'no different."

'Course it ain't, Al thought. *Not to you.*

"That's right," Marty said simply.

Benny turned towards his partner, a smirk of satisfaction on his lips. "So what's the fuckin' problem, Al?"

Al sighed heavily. "Shut up, Benny. Seriously."

"Al," Teehan warned, "don't let it get personal." His tone was flat; it was one that Al had long ago recognized as something you didn't want to hear from this man. "I get that it's the old neighborhood and all, but you're a professional, aren't you?"

Shit, Al thought.

***

Half a dozen police cruisers, lights flashing but sirens silent, parked at sharp angles to form a partition of steel at either end of the block between Elm and Cork Street. Uniformed officers stood sentry on the near side of yellow police-tape, keeping crowds of curious onlookers outside the flimsy plastic barrier. Inside of the cordon, more harness cops, crime scene technicians and members of the city coroner's staff went about their business collecting, cataloguing and tagging, photographing and noting every square inch of the scene of a double homicide committed in broad daylight.

In the midst of the chaos of an active crime-scene, Nicole Edwards — pushing middle-age, attractive but worn down by time and the stress of a thankless job — nodded and folded up the notebook she'd been writing

74

in. As she placed it in the inside pocket of the dun-colored, lightweight jacket she wore, the gold shield pinned to her belt caught the light for an instant, making it shine as if the star depicted on it was real.

"All right, Mrs. Iolescu, thank you for your time and for your help. I appreciate it."

"For what good it'll do." The old woman shook her head, watery eyes unfocused, staring past Edwards at the two deep-red stains on the concrete sidewalk almost directly in front of her apartment building. A crime-scene photographer moved between the discolored spots and the building, his back to the two women, snapping dozens of pictures from every conceivable angle.

Edwards understood how the woman felt – it was unsettling, to say the least. Before she could respond, though, Iolescu clumped heavily up the steps and back into the relative safety of the building without so much as a parting nod.

The detective let out a heavy breath, turned and found Jeff Park, her partner of three years, approaching.

"Anything?" he asked.

She tucked a strand of auburn hair, just starting to become wisped with gray, behind one ear and shook her head. "No more than anybody else. Heard two pops, then two more a moment later, then a car peeling out. And of course, she didn't see a thing."

"Figures." There was a note of gloom in Park's voice. "At least she admitted she *heard* something. Middle of the day but somehow not one person sees a thing." Hands on hips, he shook his head slowly, watching the crime-scene technicians at their work. "Does anyone *ever* own up to seeing anything?"

Edwards said, "Is that disillusionment I hear?" but was only half-listening. Park got like this occasionally. Not often – he was one of the most optimistic, cheerful cops she'd ever met. Some days she appreciated it, some days it bugged the hell out of her. Right now, she had enough on her mind, enough frustration of her own, that Park's slid right past her. Her attention was focused on the area around them, her gaze scanning, setting the scene firmly in her memory. Her thoughts churned, trying to determine what pieces around her were part of the puzzle and what should be ignored.

Park said something else, but she didn't catch it. Instead, she cut back in, saying, "This is five bodies in the last two weeks, all in the same general area."

"And we're sure they're all related?"

"Dollars to doughnuts." Edwards stepped off the stoop, headed towards the corner of Cork Street, where her parked car formed part of the blockade sealing the street from through-traffic. "The M.O. is the same: pushers killed in broad daylight, in a public place, two slugs in each, nothing taken from the victims."

Park followed at her side, looking around them intensely, as if he might suddenly somehow spot the killer or killers, hidden in plain sight or perhaps conjuring them to his side by the power of his thoughts alone. "Right. So they're pros who know exactly who they're hitting and when and where they'll be."

They stopped by the cruiser; Edwards popped open the driver's side door, but Park stood in place, his eyes roaming freely across the area. "I'd almost like to believe it was some vigilante, thinking they're doing our job for us, but—"

"No stupid-ass jokes, please. I'm not in the mood. Not when the smell of gang warfare is in the air."

Park raised his hands in surrender. "I wasn't joking. Not really. Sorry. I was going to say, I'd *like* to believe this isn't the start of some turf war, but nothing else really makes sense at this point."

"Tell me something I *don't* know." Edwards didn't bother to hide her annoyance. "Please. And I'm not joking, either."

"I can't," the other detective admitted, rubbing his stubbly chin. "But..." He pointed at a spot somewhere further down the block. "Maybe that can."

Edwards followed his gaze, but even so had no clue to what he was referring. "Okay, help me out here. What the hell are you talking about?"

"You don't see it? The security cam over that bodega?"

Edwards squinted hard and managed to just pick out the device her partner referenced, mounted over the front door of a store in the first floor of a tenement building. It pointed in the direction of an ATM off to one side of the entrance and faced the corner of Cork Street where they stood.

"Are you fucking with me? Jeff, look at it! It's so far away that it couldn't possibly..." She trailed off, then added, "How did you even *see* that thing?"

Park slipped around the front of the car, heading towards the convenience store. "I eat my veggies. C'mon, sometimes miracles do happen."

Edwards shook her head as she slammed the cruiser's door closed and turned to follow. "Lord knows I could use one."

8

Al paused, his hand on the vertical pull-bar of the metal and glass door. He tossed over his shoulder, "You let me do all the talking in here, got it?"

A cigarette bobbed up and down between Benny's lips as his eyes wandered upwards towards the weather-beaten sign reading "MAGINI'S DRUGS" that hung over the storefront, then back down to street-level. The place was old—ancient, even, to Benny's eyes—and probably hadn't been updated since it was first opened sometime in the... what? Fifties? Sixties, at least. Benny wasn't good with that sort of thing; everything old was just old as far as he was concerned. Who cared about when it was new? But this place took the cake. Everything about it was penny-ante and rundown. Even the yellowed, ornately handwritten "OPEN" sign hanging in the front door seemed ancient and cheap to him. What was the point in keeping a dump like this open, he wondered. Better to burn it to the ground and start over again.

"Sure thing," he said, plucking the cigarette from his lips before flicking it contemptuously against the store's wide front window, adding, "Boss," with barely concealed sarcasm.

Al grimaced at his reflection in the glass, but let it slide. He hauled the heavy door open and stepped into the cool, brightly lit interior of the drugstore, setting off a tiny, electronic chime as he set foot on the thick, rubber doormat inside.

The sound of the chime was followed almost immediately by a cheerful voice from somewhere deeper in the building: "Hello! Good afternoon! I'll be right with you in just a moment!"

The place was long and narrow, essentially a hallway equal in length to the depth of the building, though less than a third as wide as it was long. The walls were lined with shelves crammed full of over-the-counter medicines of every stripe, toiletries, household goods and a scattering of dry-grocery items, like cereal and snacks. The druggist's counter was situated against the back wall and, next to it, was the cashier register. Before these stood a pair of old-fashioned wire spinner-racks, one stuffed with greeting cards and one with magazines, comic books, and cheap paperback novels, each with a tier of its own. Nostalgia nipped at the back of Al's mind every time he set foot in this store. From day to day, visit to visit, it looked exactly the same as it always did. Little had changed since he'd shopped — and occasionally shoplifted — here as a kid. In a way, there was comfort in that, but it also made these stops a hell of a lot harder to stomach.

Benny followed three or four paces behind him, eyes sliding over the products on display, broadcasting boredom and disdain. A fresh, unlit, cigarette bobbed from his lower lip. His gaze caught on something for a moment and he snorted – whether in amusement or disgust wasn't clear.

Al cast a surreptitious glance at the young man, satisfied that he seemed to be behaving himself, for now at least. Let him think whatever he wanted about Magini's. Didn't matter a bit. Al approached the counter. Benny split off, moved towards the magazine rack, spinning it lazily, glancing at titles and covers. He plucked a comic book with a brightly colored cover from the spinner and began to leaf through it.

From a doorway set in the wall on the opposite side of the counter appeared a small man with a big, friendly smile, his slate gray hair and mustache perfectly trimmed and combed, his pale blue eyes bright and alert. He wore a red apron over a white, button-down shirt, a bowtie nestled at his collar. The ensemble made the old man look like he'd stepped not only out of some previous era, but another place entirely – a more innocent one, maybe, where people like Al and Benny would never have even met people like him.

"What can I do for you tod—" the little man began, before his eyes registered who it was that stood on the other side of the counter. His smile evaporated and the luster went out of his eyes. He grew even smaller, as if trying to hide within himself. "Oh. It's you. How are you today, Al?"

Al kept his own face carefully neutral – putting on the expression of the "professional" Marty had felt it necessary to remind him that he was. "C'mon, Mister Magini. Don't be coy."

"All right then." Magini gave up any pretense of pleasantries, his face closing off to form a mask that failed to hide his true thoughts. Even as he brought it out, the facade threatened to break under the pressure of whatever he was holding back. "I – I don't have the money for you, Al."

"Are you fuckin' kiddin' me?" came the growl from behind Al. Benny moved next to his senior partner, slamming a fist down on the counter, making both a display of brochures about high blood-pressure and the druggist himself jump. "You *owe* you *pay*. That's the way it God-damned works, old man. What kinda shit you tryin' ta pull?"

"Benny!" Al barked, short and sharp, hand balling into a fist, clenched tightly at waist level.

The younger man paid no attention, his focus on Magini as his lips curled into a menacing tough guy snarl he'd probably practiced in the mirror. And it worked – on Magini, at least. The smaller man seemed to shrink even more under Benny's glare.

With effort, Al unclenched his fist and inserted himself between Benny and the wooden counter, edging the younger man away with an elbow, keeping one eye on Magini as he did.

"Back off," he snarled, half under his breath, before turning to face the shopkeeper again. "He *is* right, though, Mister Magini. You do owe and you're way behind in your payments."

Magini was frightened; his heart pounded against his breastbone and his eyes darted between the faces of the two men. He felt Benny's scowling gaze on him as if it had physical weight. Weight enough to crush him. With his own eyes he implored Al for whatever help he could give. Magini had once thought of Al as intimidating, but the calm, simmering threat he posed now seemed like the lesser evil. Compared to this new one, Al was almost easygoing. Al wanted to collect the money Magini had borrowed from his boss – that was all. The druggist didn't dare think about what the younger man really wanted to do.

The devil you know, he thought, wishing it were so.

"I know, Al. I know," Magini began. "I'm sorry, but—" He held up his hands, helplessly, as if showing the other men that they were empty, that he had nothing to give them. "I... I..." He trailed off, then broke down, his voice cracking, tears gathering in the corners of his eyes.

"I know you don't care." Magini raised his hands to his face, hiding his fear and shame from these men whom he was sure not only didn't care, but couldn't understand. "But business is so slow," he continued. "I can't compete with the chain stores. I only took that loan from Mister Castella to keep my head above water and—"

"And it made things worse," Al finished for him.

Magini was surprised. He peeked through parted fingers at the other man, allowed himself a glimmer of hope in the unexpected sympathy he heard in Al's voice. "Yes... that's it, exactly. It was a mistake. I realize that now."

"I don't fuckin' *believe* this!" Benny exploded, throwing out an openhanded push that sent the rack of books and magazines he'd been browsing earlier crashing to the floor, scattering its contents. "Are you actually *fallin'* for this sad-sack bullshit?!"

Al spun on his heel, stepped forward, jabbed a finger into Benny's face. "Get the fuck outside," he growled, voice modulated for Benny's ears only. "And wait for me."

Batting Al's finger away, Benny spat, "Why you takin' *his* side, Al? Cuz this is your old neighborhood? So fuckin' what? You forget what Teehan said?"

Al grabbed the lapels of Benny's crisp, white sports coat, pulling him closer so the men's faces were only inches apart. He spat, "Get outside. *Now.* I won't tell you again." Then he spun Benny on his heels and shoved him, hard, in the direction of the entrance, forcing the somewhat smaller man to move forward at an awkward stumble or lose his balance.

A step before he reached the door, Benny looked over his shoulder towards where Al stood glowering. The youth's face burned red in a volatile mixture of fury and shame. He opened the door, then pulled it shut behind him as hard as the pneumatic closing-device would allow, making a muted *fwump* sound.

Magini was pale, his breath coming hard and fast as he leaned on the wooden counter for support. "Th-thank you, Al. I—"

Al turned, stone-faced. "One more week. That's all I can manage. Even I can't disappoint or say no to Castella for long, so you better have something for him by then. For both of our sakes. I like you Mister Magini, I do – but not *that* much."

Al headed towards the door, following after Benny.

"Al."

He stopped, but did not look back.

"I appreciate this, what you've done for me," Magini continued. "And I'm glad it's you here and not—"

"Don't even finish that thought, Mister Magini."

Magini screwed up what little courage he had left. Shaking his head, heedless of what Al had said, he continued: "This business has been in my family for almost sixty years, Al. It's my own fault I'm in this mess, but if it wasn't for you and your kindness, this would already be nothing more than a memory."

"Kindness has got nothin' to do with it. And this may all still come crashin' down on our heads. Don't forget that."

The tinny, electronic chime sounded again as Al exited the store. In the twenty-eight years Stuart Magini operated the store since his father's passing, it had never sounded anything other than bright and cheery to his ears. At that moment, he couldn't imagine anything more ominous.

9

Al allowed the door to close gently behind him. He was furious, but there was no point in throwing tantrums. Benny's was plenty for both of them. Trying to remind Al to be a professional and then acting like a fucking toddler was Benny all over.

Al looked left and right, scanning the streets and sidewalk, but there was no sign of the kid.

"Where the hell did he run off to?" Al muttered. "Did he not hear what I fuckin' told him?"

He rubbed his temples, dreading the headache he could feel coming, as his own words came back to him: *Even I can't disappoint or say no to Castella for long.*

***

"Am I hearing things right? Are you saying 'no' to me, Al?"

"No, sir." *Shit. Wrong way to put that.*

The interior of Eduardo Castella's private lounge was a wide, dimly-lit room of wooden paneling, overstuffed leather chairs and expensive, if smoke-stained, pieces of artwork. At twenty-seven years old, Al Vacarro had already been a "soldier" for Castella for more than a third of his life, and a made man before he'd even turned eighteen. He'd been in this room any number of times, standing before Castella as he did now, or even sometimes sitting in one of those chairs, enjoying a cigar from Castella's own humidor, the walnut one with the fancy "C" embossed in it that had belonged to Castella's old man. Surrounded by friends and comrades, a cigar in one hand and a snifter of something in the other, it always seemed like a warm and friendly place.

Now…

Well. Al knew his way around, and that he had proven himself. He knew, too, that, in his own way, Castella liked him. Even so, it was smart to always step lightly. Especially when he'd stepped in it.

Al waved his hand casually, as if trying to erase his faux pas. "What I'm trying to say, sir," he began again, "is that I don't think it's necessary. With all due respect, of course," he added quickly.

"Are you tellin' me," Castella said quietly, cold fury plain evidence that Al's second attempt at an explanation had made things worse, "what is and isn't necessary for my business?"

Al's heart skipped a beat and his palms began to dampen. *Tread lightly, kiddo*, he reminded himself.

"I would never dare, Mister Castella, sir," he said, ignoring the fact that he already had. "But if you'll, uh, indulge me a minute here, please do me this favor and consider that this ain't a Ronnie situation."

Castella plucked a smoldering cigar from the heavy, black and white, stone ashtray perched on the edge of the table near his elbow, took a puff, then another, his eyes boring into Al as he considered. Castella leaned forward, shifting to the edge of the deep, richly plush chair, the expensive material of his suit straining over a belly that had begun to bulge the last few years, swollen by excess and stress. Less than a decade earlier, Eddie Castella had inherited from his father a vast, thriving business empire, one built over nearly half a century through careful planning, pledges of loyalty from numerous smaller organizations, and judicious use of violence. And for most of his life, the younger Castella had been there, too, watching, learning at his father's knee. He had seen everything his father could have shown him about this world they lived in. He should have been prepared for the position he found himself in when Nunzio Castella unexpectedly passed. But the state of the business over the last several years proved otherwise. Some of those lessons Eddie's father had tried to instill in him still hadn't settled in, but he was trying. In this thing of theirs, it was literally do or die.

This was Castella trying. "A favor…" he said slowly. "Well, go on, then."

"Okay." Al surreptitiously wiped his sweating palms against his pant-legs and took a deep breath. "Ronnie was snitching, and you said it was obvious, right? Police raids, business down, a sloppy trail leading back to him and he wasn't even gettin' anythin' from it, right?" Al had repeated that story to himself so often it had become something like fact. His own part in the story, he tried not to remember.

"Yeah," Castella allowed. "And what's your point?"

"My point is that this ain't nothin' like that. None of that stuff has happened since, right? It's been years. So there's nothin' to really worry about is what I'm saying. We could let it end. We could just let this one go."

The gangster reached over, stubbing the half-smoked cigar out forcefully, angrily, in the ashtray, grinding it down into a stubby nub, causing the wrappings to split and spill unsmoked tobacco.

"How many people you taken care of for me over the years you worked for me, Al?" he asked, eyes on the ruined cigar.

Unsure where the question was leading, Al answered cautiously, "I don't know, Mister Castella. A few."

Castella's eyes met the younger man's. "More than a few and you never said boo about any of 'em to me before—not since Ronnie, anyway—so I know you must feel strongly about this, Al."

Al nodded slightly. "Yeah. I do. Sir."

Castella leaned back in the chair again, placing his arms flat on the rests, gaze drifting away from Al towards some point on the ceiling. "I admire strong convictions. And I admire the balls it takes to argue with me, even if it pisses me off when people do it. Rare as it is, I should add." He paused for a carefully calculated moment, then his eyes met Al's again, pinning his subordinate in place through sheer willpower. He stared hard at Al, long enough that the younger man began to worry again. "Al, let's not make a habit of it, hmm?"

Al said, "No, sir," shaking his head. He mentally kicked himself for choosing those words yet again.

Castella ignored it. He stared at the other man for a long moment. He asked, "Do you know what happens when you save a life, Al?" He levered himself from the chair, moved to stand before Al, never breaking eye-contact. "You take responsibility for it. It's a kind of relationship just as important as family. Maybe *more* important, since you choose to bring it on yourself. And like family, it never ends. As long as you're alive and on this Earth, that responsibility remains. Are you ready for an obligation like that?"

Al's mouth and palms suddenly seemed very dry. He swallowed hard before answering.

***

Al groaned and rubbed the bridge of his nose with two fingers. Lost in thought, he hadn't moved ten feet from the front of Magini's store. He didn't know how long he'd stood there.

That kid is gonna be the death of me. The thought had lodged itself in his brain and wouldn't let go.

The conversation with Jenna the night before came back to him, along with twinges of guilt about the way he'd left things with her. He couldn't let himself worry about it, though. He'd said, *He's gonna take someone down and it's probably going to be me.* He had only reluctantly admitted it, in a moment when his guard was relaxed, but once he said it out loud, it was hard not to think of it every time Benny did something stupid or impetuous. The kid was more trouble than he would ever be worth. There was no way he could ever tell Castella that, though, much less make him see it for himself.

Al walked the short distance to where he'd parked the car, around the nearest corner and a little ways down the next block, hoping Benny had simply decided to wait for him there.

There was no sign of him. Because of course there wouldn't be.

"Fuck it." Al said, opening the driver's side and sliding behind the wheel. The big, eight-cylinder engine turned over with a roar and eased out into the light, early afternoon traffic. "Mike's should be open and I sure as shit could use a cold one."

***

"So, I'm really sorry I couldn't get him to clear it with you first, Mister," *Mist-uh*, "Castella, but you get how it is sometimes…" The contrition in Benny's voice almost sounded sincere.

Without breaking stride on the running machine, Eddie Castella cast a glance over his shoulder towards where the young man, hands fig-leafed before him in a show of false bashfulness, stood. Castella turned back towards the wall of glass on the opposite side of his home gym, flicking sweat out of his eyes with a shake of the head.

When he was young, people called Eddie Castella "Handsome Eddie" or "Fast Eddie." Why not? He had been handsome and he was a man who loved all of life's pleasures. Life was for living, after all, and he didn't care to be stingy when it came to indulging himself, whether that indulgence was food, wine or women. A couple of decades of living that sweet life, and a few blows to the business that had lost him a significant chunk of the territory his father had carved out of this city — as well as the accompanying respect—had earned him another nickname: "Fat Eddie." He didn't like it, but he could live with it. What did he care what people called him, as long as he was still making money? And then came the stroke. It was minor, and recovery was swift, but with it came a determined viciousness that he hadn't possessed even as a young man. Eddie Castella dedicated himself to his health and restoring his empire. Now, after shedding nearly a hundred pounds and silencing half a dozen rivals to his power in the last three years, people usually called him "Mister Castella" or just "sir." Regardless of his age or weight or appearance, nobody had ever called him a fool or taken him for one. Not and lived to regret it.

"Save it," he interrupted, cutting Benny's story short. "I don't like what I'm hearing here, boy," he emphasized the last word, putting the kid in his place. "Al Vacarro's been with me a good long time. And his daddy before him, you know. I've had doubts about Al from time to time, even butted heads with him once or twice. He gets these ideas..." Snatches of conversations over the years flitted through his brain, little birds whispering things he didn't want to hear. "Hell, I've wanted to smack him around now and then, but he always comes through in the end," he continued. "By and large, Al Vacarro's been a good guy to have around. A good *soldier*."

With theatrical exaggeration, Benny chimed in, playing along. "Oh, yes, sir, I understand that and I was as shocked as you. But I gotta say, you haven't seen Al up close and personal these last few weeks the way I have. I get that you put me in with him to show me the ropes, but I still don't know jack about your operation. He hasn't taught me hardly nothin' at all. He treats me like some kid he's babysittin'. But even I can see that the way Al handles himself, it's like he don't even care about your money. He's given this old guy Magini extensions on his loan left and right and I don't see that the guy's payin' anythin' at all anymore. That just don't seem right to me."

Castella clicked off the running machine with a swipe of his finger and stepped down, accepting a towel from Martin Teehan. Teehan had, reluctantly, escorted Benny into the don's inner sanctum, but damned if he was going to leave them alone. Possibly the kid was as stupid as he seemed, possibly it was all an act. Either way, he could still be dangerous. There should be eyes on him at all times.

"Well," Castella turned towards Benny, his expression contemplative. "It's true that Al's collections have been way down the last few months. Don't know why he still insists on doin' 'em himself.

These small-time loans ain't even worth the hassle. A man like Al Vacarro should be usin' his talents elsewhere." Castella turned from the young man, shaking his head slowly, a note of anger coming into his voice. "And he *has* made excuses for this Magini fella before. More than once. Who the fuck is this guy that Al should care so much? Say... Marty, that's the old neighborhood, isn't it? Where Magini's is?" He cast a glance at Teehan, who nodded confirmation.

Benny's head bobbed. "Yeah, I think it might be."

"I wasn't asking *you*," Castella snapped.

"It's true I ain't personally seen Al at work in a long time," Castella continued, wiping sweat from his forehead with the workout towel. "And it has always struck me as strange that he still likes to do collections himself. I mean, he's no *goomba* slappin' street-leather after all these years. He could have guys doin' that things like that. He *should* have them, matter of fact. I don't know why he doesn't. But what I do know is that he ain't bringing in my money like he's supposed to be." Castella sighed. "I hate feeling like this. I just fuckin' hate it, but trust is a fragile thing, isn't it?"

"Yes, sir," Benny agreed, allowing himself a grin. "And trust is all you got, right? I mean, it ain't like there's any blood between you and him."

"Don't you fuckin' *push* me, kid." Castella snapped each of the words off like he was biting them off of the end of something acrid – something harsher that he'd rather have said. He turned towards Marty. "What do you think?"

"Al's got stuff on his mind these days." Marty's expression and tone made it clear the entire conversation was distasteful, but he could hardly refuse to answer. "No idea what it is, but he's been... distracted. Maybe he ain't up to snuff in his work, but he's got history and he *does* have blood." His eyes flickered towards Benny then away. "He's one of us. Has been since the day he was born. If it were up to me, Eddie, I'd give him the benefit of the doubt, give him a little leeway. Have a talk with him if it goes on too much longer."

Behind Castella's back, safely out of the old man's view, Benny grinned evilly at the don's chief *capo* and said, "But it ain't up to you."

Castella whirled on his heel with a speed that belied his age, his hand flying out to whip an openhanded blow across Benny's face with a *crack* like sudden thunder. "What did I fuckin' *say*, not even a *minute* ago, you little shit?"

In shocked surprise, Benny raised a hand to his reddening cheek, then caught himself, bowed his head and backed up a step. "I'm sorry, Mister Castella. I got a big mouth and I don't think sometimes. I shouldn't have said nothin'. I'm real sorry."

"Learn to keep that trap closed or I'll close it for you then send you back where you fuckin' came from. You're here as a favor and don't you fuckin' forget it." Castella looked sideways at Benny as he returned his attention to the waiting Teehan. "Doubts are one thing, Marty, but evidence is another and I know for sure that Al has been playin' fast and loose with my money where this Magini fuck is concerned. He plays loose once, he'll do it again. And even the thought makes me itchy, if you know what I mean." A snarl in his voice now, he continued, "You said he's got things on his mind? That he's 'distracted'? That makes me wonder. It *really* makes me wonder what else he's been up to. Could be he might even know somethin' about those little 'leaks' we were talkin' about the other night."

Castella grunted, tossed the sweaty towel onto the front bar of the exercise machine. The anger seemed to drain from him as quickly as it had come and his eyes went distant with thought. He gripped the machine's rubber-wrapped handles tightly, his knuckles going white with the effort. "Marty, I hate like hell to say it, but I think I got to take what this loudmouthed punk's saying seriously."

Teehan said nothing. He kept his eyes on Castella and his mouth shut. He didn't like where the conversation was going, but when Castella got like this, there was no use trying to talk to him.

Benny tried to keep his composure, but it was hard to hide the delight flitting around inside his brain, making his stomach sprout butterflies at the prospect of vengeance for the slights he'd suffered these last few weeks. "Thanks a lot, sir. I appreciate the confidence. And don't you worry, Mister Castella, I'll make sure to put this right. I didn't wanna do nothin' without your say so, but I think I got an idea how to get Al's head back in the game. You know, put a fire in his belly and get him walkin' the straight and narrow again."

Castella turned, his face tight and eyes sharply focused as he looked Benny straight on. "Fine. You do that. We'll let this be a test of your own aptitude. You make Al see what side his bread's buttered on and make sure he does the job he's been tasked with, the way he knows it should be done. After that, after everything's been put right, you bring him back here. We'll have ourselves a chat and see if we can all be a happy little family again."

He took a step closer to the young man. "You better be on the level about this, though," he said, his voice lowering and becoming raspy, giving Benny a glimpse of the man Eddie Castella must have been in his youth, before decadence and age took their toll. "I will not tolerate people fucking with my money, but I also won't tolerate lying or half-assed bullshit, either. *Capische*?"

Without another word or a backwards glance, Castella made for the door on the far side of the room. Teehan remained a moment or two longer, gave Benny a meaningful look and then followed his boss.

Benny just grinned.

10

Al Vacarro never got drunk. He drank regularly – he enjoyed a few beers or a couple shots of whiskey, or a glass of wine sometimes on special occasions, like those increasingly rare nights out with Lexi or a meal with the important members of the Organization. But he knew his limits and he stayed well within them. Drinking wasn't entertainment to him, it was a release, a way to shed some of the stress that knotted the muscles in his back and twisted his guts. He didn't need to get drunk to achieve that, and more than that, he feared the loss of the control, the possibility of saying or doing something he'd regret.

He wasn't missing anything. He'd gotten drunk before – well and truly, senses lost, dead to the world drunk. And once was enough.

***

On Al Vacarro's twenty-first birthday, he decided he would like a drink. Why not? It was the first day he could legally drink a beer or a shot while standing at a bar like a man, instead of a twelve-year-old kid sneaking a beer out of his parents' refrigerator to drink in the park, passed among friends. Or like a ragged, seventeen-year-old "soldier" in the backroom of his boss's restaurant, gulping straight from a bottle, trying to quiet the shaking in his hands from a night of "work" that he'd never imagined needed doing.

On his twenty-first birthday, on Eddie Castella's dime, Al Vacarro got roaring drunk.

He hadn't exactly planned it that way.

When Castella invited him, and his cousin Mike, and a few of the other young men in his employ, out to celebrate Al's birthday, he'd been proud. Eduardo Castella, the all-powerful head of the family, made time for *Al* – a nobody, just a grunt in a large and far-flung organization. He didn't kid himself, though; it was because of Eddie's friendship with his father. Even after close to five years, Al still felt like he was living in Tony's shadow. Maybe he always would. But he worked hard, he followed orders, did the best he could every damned day, and maybe that was finally getting close to being enough. It was possible, he hoped, that Eddie had even come to recognize Al on his own merits.

And that's why Al decided that he wouldn't get drunk. The last thing he wanted was to say or do something to embarrass himself in front of Castella. Or worse, insult the man.

When the six men, dressed in their best suits—Al's brand-new, precisely tailored, a birthday gift to himself—and highly polished shoes, entered the neon dimness of the Cockatoo Club cocktail lounge, its patrons parted around them without even realizing they were doing so. The place drew a lively crowd: cool-eyed women in short, flashy dresses and men who thought they were slick; singles of all sizes and shapes looking for a good time and couples who hadn't forgotten how to have one. The wide, busy room was filled with loud music and spirited conversation. But men carrying themselves in a certain way commanded respect, regardless of the company they found themselves in, and it was nearly impossible not to recognize that in this small group.

They appropriated a suddenly available table in a corner of the lounge, and one of them—a guy who always introduced himself as "Louis," but everyone called Lou regardless—grabbed a passing waitress to place their orders. For two hours, their glasses emptied and filled, first with shots, then with beers, and conversation veered from topic to topic, pushed by the conflicting waves of youthful interests and vigor and more life-experience among them than half of the room combined could claim. Loves and lies and plans and jokes flew around as their brains soaked up alcohol and their tensions melted away. Girls approached singly or in pairs, flirting and teasing, settling onto one lap or another, scamming drinks and pushing napkins with probably-fake phone numbers into pockets before drifting back into the crowd with giggles and promises and winks and sultry looks. It was all a game; everyone knew the rules and nobody expected anything more or anything less.

Al drank slowly, savoring what was put before him, never getting more than the contact-high from his half-drunk friends around him, but having a great time all the same. He looked around the table at the familiar faces as they smiled, laughed, jeered, argued. He had never felt out of place among them, but he hadn't realized until that night just how much he belonged with them, either. The cares, the trials, the stress of the past few years all of a sudden seemed like nothing at all. He couldn't imagine what other path his life might have taken and he'd have almost gladly done it all over again. Some moments were darker than others, but the light of those others more than made up for it.

The plan for the night had been to have a few drinks here at the lounge—a place chosen at random, where new faces could be met, anonymously and without risk—before moving on to one of the "gentlemen's clubs" that Castella had "inherited" from a former competitor. But plans never held together in the face of reality and as women kept approaching the table, either drawn by the aura that surrounded these hard-eyed, easy-laughing young men or by the freeness with which Castella was spending money, it wasn't long before members of the group began to leave the table with them.

Mike was the first. Easing the giggling redhead from his lap and back onto her own two feet, he stood, grinned at his cousin, half apologetically and half lecherously, and said, "Gonna go, uh, check the weather. Be back in a while," earning a round of catcalls and encouragement from the crew.

Al nodded, grinned back. "Hey, sure, enjoy. Just don't forget an umbrella in case it rains." Mike barked a laugh, slapped his new friend's perky rear and hurried her towards a side exit.

And so it went, various retreads of the same scene. It was as if Mike, in working up the courage to abandon the man of the hour, had set the others free to do the same. Al didn't mind; let 'em have fun. A party was for the guests and he'd be doing the same if he didn't have his eye on someone already. He thought of the curvy little blonde with the big brown eyes working the front desk of one of Castella's legitimate businesses — a soft-drink bottling plant — and smiled to himself. Maybe he wasn't yet anything to her, but she meant something to him. He just had to prove that to the girl.

"Somethin' on your mind?" In the raucous space, in that wide open room filled with sound and moving bodies, the voice was so close and so clear that it seemed loud, even through the noise.

Al let the smile fade to a grin. "Nah, Mister Castella. Just enjoyin' myself. I gotta thank you for tonight."

Eddie Castella clomped his chair around in a half-turn so he that he could speak more directly to Al. He rattled the ice in his empty glass, made a face. "It ain't over yet, son. You're only gettin' started."

Son. Castella had called him that off and on for years. He never thought anything of it before, but now there was something weighty in the way he said it, even in the casual context in which the word was used.

Al looked at the other man. Really looked. Castella probably wasn't too far past forty. No more than forty-five, tops. Only a little more than twice Al's age. His hair was still thick and black, his face mostly unlined, except for a few places around those sharp, dark eyes. But in those eyes... even through the beginnings of the hearty drunkenness that Castella was cultivating, even past the bright intelligence that shone there, even through the emotional mask that a man in his position never really put aside, there was something that stood out. A quality Al couldn't quite place. But one thing was obvious: there was something Eddie Castella wanted to say.

"Hey, boss... Mister Castella. Something on your mind?"

Castella made a noncommittal sound – a sort of grunting snort. He reached across the table for an abandoned, half-filled beer mug, drained it, set it back down. His suit-coat straining over the belly he was beginning to develop, he leaned back in his chair, said, "You guys... you guys got so much ahead of you. I envy the shit out of you some days."

Al didn't know what response Castella was looking for, so he said nothing.

That was fine. Castella needed no prompting. "None of you young guys—you're barely more'n kids, really—know what life is. This thing we do, this thing of ours... it's the Life, capital "el," sure as hell, but it ain't *life*. It's money and power and danger and sometimes it's just plain *fun*, but what does it get you?"

Al waited, but Castella went quiet, saying nothing more, simply staring sullenly at his subordinate. The man seemed to want an actual answer to his question.

"Respect," Al ventured, aware that he was on dangerous ground. "At least from me. From us, I mean," he added.

"Sure," Castella nodded slowly. "Sure, when I'm tossin' money around or got a gun to your head, you'll respect me all I want. Anybody would. Can't blame nobody for that." Castella picked up and waved an empty glass towards a passing waitress. The woman nodded acknowledgment but didn't stop. Castella made a disgusted sound.

Al shook his head. "Nah, it ain't like that. It's—"

"It *is*," Castella snapped, spitting out the words like they were something hard and bitter. Less harshly, he said, "For most of 'em. Not you, Al. Your cousin's a good boy, too. He's not a bright boy, not like you, but he's a loyal boy. That's important cuz you guys know... you guys came from the right place. You know where your head should be, who takes care of you. These other shits..." he sighed then looked around. "Where's that fuckin' waitress?"

Castella rubbed his hands across his eyes. "What the fuck am I sayin'?"

"'S'okay, Mister Castella, I understand."

"No, you don't." Castella breathed deeply, as if oxygen would clear the haze from his thoughts and set them into the proper order. "What I'm sayin' is, don't be like me. Don't let *this* life be *your* life. You hear me?"

Al's head bobbed, once, twice. "Sure, Mister Castella."

"Don't 'sure' me, Al." Castella's eyes met the younger man's, bored through him, all traces of the drunken wistfulness he'd been lost in suddenly gone. "I mean it. Think about what I said and make sure you *really* heard me. Your pop was real important to me, Al. The best friend I ever had. He made some mistakes. I made some mistakes. But it never changed that we were friends. The end he came to brought me to tears. Honest to God, when I heard, I cried for Tony. I didn't cry for my own father."

The look on Castella's face somehow scared Al now. There was an intensity, and an honesty, that Al had never seen – not in anyone.

"And Tony," the older man continued, "he never asked me to, but, when he... passed, I promised myself I'd steer you straight, Al. Make sure you're headed in the right direction. I don't wanna see you get the shit the way your dad did. Since he went, my pop did, too, and now, I feel like you're the closest thing I got to family. No good uncle and braindead Jersey cousins a-fuckin'-side." He sighed. "Listen, don't take it as anythin' weird, but I care about you, kid. That's what I'm tryin' to say."

Stunned by Castella's emotional outpour, all the younger man could manage was, "Thanks, Mister Castella."

Castella nodded, apparently satisfied.

The waitress chose that moment to reappear. "Sorry, sweetie, busy night. You want another round?"

Castella glanced at the woman out of the corner of his eye, ran his tongue along the sharp edge of his incisors, then looked back towards

Al and said, "You know, I think I'm done after all. Sorry, Al, but I'm gonna call it a night."

"No problem, Mister Castella. Let me call your car for you."

Castella stood, waving Al's offer away with a slightly wobbly hand. "I'm fine. I'm a grown-ass man. I can call for a God-damned car myself." He dug in his pocket, pulled out a wad of cash and shoved it towards the woman, who still stood nearby, looking miffed but mystified at being hailed then dismissed. "Here. For the table and yourself. Whatever's left over." He shook his head, short and sharp like a dog shedding water, stood up straight and walked towards the door without a trace of unsteadiness, as if he hadn't been drinking for the last two-plus hours.

Reeling at the revelations he'd been handed, unsure of how to process either the information or the sentiment behind them, Al sat alone at a table for six, surrounded by empty glasses and empty noise that flowed around him like the current in a fast-moving stream around a solitary stone.

"Well?" the waitress cut in on his thoughts, gesturing with the wad of Castella's cash she still held.

"Shit, I don't know," Al admitted. He looked around the room at the people chatting, flirting, dancing, drinking, living. "Round for everyone, I guess, and bring a bottle here."

"A bottle of...?" the girl prompted, impatiently.

"Somethin' that burns," Al said vaguely. "I got a lot to think about."

11

Late morning had rolled over into early afternoon. The heat the day had earlier promised hadn't yet materialized and the afternoon was instead turning out to be comfortably warm with a pleasant breeze keeping the true heat at bay. Inside the East Street Bar, though, it was dim and cool no matter the time or weather. The dirty, dark-tinted windows contributed, but the borderline squalor was what made it stick.

It wasn't yet two o'clock and the place didn't do food, so while it was open, since there was no lunch crowd, it was hardly busy this early in the day. The customary barflies were scattered around the place, the kind you'll find anywhere in the world that man has invented alcohol or figured out how to import it: men with nowhere to be and nowhere they'd *like* to be other than the bottom of a bottle. Seated at tiny stained, rough-hewn tables or occupying one of the dozen and a half stools at the long, scarred bar that took up nearly the full length of the place's eastern wall, most of the bar's patrons were silent except for the occasional clink of a glass on a table or counter, the irregular squeak of a stool swiveling or footsteps moving in the direction of the john.

Behind the bar, dully glowing beer neons did their best to brighten the atmosphere, but succeeded only in sending multi-colored, shimmering lights through the bottles of liquor adorning the spaces beneath and between them. Sandwiched between the wall of bottles and the bar itself, Michael Costa, dressed in a tight black t-shirt that strained against well-toned arms, and a pair of stained, well-worn jeans, used the edge of his once-white apron to polish a stubborn mark from the rim of a pint-glass. As he worked, he nodded or grunted agreement when expected, as his cousin—the only one in the bar at the moment who was using his mouth for anything but drinking—talked.

Al finished what he had to say, then gulped down more than half of the lukewarm beer in front of him. He'd ignored the glass during the telling of his story—a carefully edited version of the last few hours' events—but now it seemed like all the talking had parched him.

"Yeah..." Mike said. "Sounds rough. Sounds like this kid is a real handful. But that's the job right now, yeah?"

Al didn't answer. He looked at his cousin, his expression saying he expected something more than superficial sympathy. He sipped the beer again, more slowly this time.

Sighing, Mike set the pint-glass on the shelf beneath the bar, satisfied that it was as clean as it was going to get. "What do you want me to tell you, Al? I hear you. It sucks. But I don't have a magic wand."

"I dunno, man. It's just..." Al leaned back from the bar, pushing against it with the palms of his hands, stretching out long fingers before him, seemingly fascinated by the interplay of light and shadow over the muscles and tendons as they moved. The word "*fragile*" inexplicably came to mind.

Al let out a short, groaning breath, leaned his elbows on the bar once more, his hands balling into frustrated fists before him. "It's all been gettin' to me the last couple of years. The boss and me used to be tight, real close, now he treats me like I'm just hired help. I'm not even sure what's changed between us, you know? But I was already gettin' tired of it all and then along comes this dumbass kid, Benny. If he's the next generation, I want no part of it. None whatsoever."

He quickly drained the remainder of his beer, as if the action could somehow put distance between himself and the dangerous thoughts he'd finally said aloud. He set the glass back on the little cardboard beermat before him as Mike settled a bottle of scotch onto the counter with a dull *clunk*.

He waggled two shot-glasses between himself and Al, one each on his index and middle fingers. "Shot?"

"Nah, it's still early. I'll take another beer, though."

Mike shrugged, pulled another draft into Al's glass from one of the taps beneath the counter, set it before his cousin and then poured two shots from the whiskey bottle. He downed one immediately as Al reached for the freshly filled pint, froth sloshing over the edge to dribble down the side of the glass.

"Look, Al," Mike said, his voice made husky by the whiskey burn. "I'm your cousin and I love you like a brother, but I don't have any answers for you. Not any you'll want to hear, anyway." He sipped from the second shot-glass, this time savoring the texture of the scorching liquid on his tongue and again as it trickled down his throat to settle in his belly. He gave himself a moment to allow its warmth to spread through him before continuing. "Besides," he said finally, "you got a lot more experience with these things than I do."

"I know." Al swirled the beer around the glass, looking down into the amber suds with suddenly bleary eyes. "I know that and I know what I want. I've just been tryin' to avoid thinkin' about it, much less saying it."

Mike leaned an elbow on the bar, coming down to eye level with Al. "Yeah?" He was genuinely curious.

Al's eyes met Mike's and the weight of the world seemed to be balanced in the heft of his gaze. He looked tired, Mike thought – not just worn out, but worn *down*.

"I want out," Al said quietly.

Mike stood straight again, scoffing, incredulous. A snort of derision burst from his nose as one side of his long, drooping mustache curled upwards with his lip. "Like it's that easy."

"Why can't it be?" Al grit his teeth, bit his cheek, then added: "*You* got out." It was half statement, half accusation.

Mike shook his head slowly. "I got *pinched*, Al. Big difference." He bared his teeth in a grimace that was equal parts frustration and anger at the memories that began to race before his mind's eye. "And when I was inside, I kept my mouth shut. Four long—*long*—years I was like a damned mute." The big man made a gesture like he was closing a zipper across his lips. "Not a word." He threw up his hands, gesturing in wide, slow arcs as if to show the enormity of his struggle. "And the cops and the D.A. and everybody else knew who I was hooked up with, even if they couldn't prove it, and they offered me all sorts of crazy deals to roll over. *Sweet* deals, if I'm honest, but I like living, you know?"

"But you did it. You got *out*," Al pressed.

"Yeah, I got out." Mike's tone had shifted to open anger. Did his cousin not understand what he was trying to say?

"I got out and then 'they' came looking for me the very same day that I was let out of stir, Al. You got no idea how hard it was to convince them to let me walk away, to convince them to leave me alone. I kept my mouth shut, sweated it out, but I honest to God thought they were gonna kill me, anyway, for a couple hours there."

Al shook his head. "No. I do know. A little, anyway. Castella was sorry to see you go. It was more about that than anything else, I think. He asked me to talk to you, but I didn't want to get involved in… in pulling you back in." Al paused, eyes searching his cousin's, looking for the other man's reaction. "Not if that was what you really wanted. Walking away from it, I mean," he added.

Are you ready to take on that obligation? Castella had asked him.

"I kinda guessed as much and I appreciate it, man. I do." Producing a rag from a pocket of his apron, Mike began to wipe down the bar's already-clean surface, trying to keep busy. Trying to tamp down the anger and frustration, Al realized. Something he himself was doing a lot of lately.

"But I still had to swear 'til I was blue in the face, under pain of death, cross my heart and *know* I'll die, not to say a word about some of the stuff I have in my head," Mike continued. "After four years, I guess you could say I had a track record they could trust."

"Listen, I know all that. But it *worked*," Al insisted. "It worked and you're out and you're *free*."

Mike straightened, swept a hand through the air, indicating the dive bar and its inhabitants. "Yeah, freedom, Al. Ain't it sweet."

"But you fuckin' *did it*!" Al snapped, shooting to his feet. His tone was sharper than he'd intended and his voice loud enough to draw looks from several drunks. He stared the nearest one down, waiting until the other man's focus returned to the drink he was nursing, before settling back onto the barstool. He returned his attention to his cousin. His voice lowered, he said, "That's my point, Mike. You got out. It can be done. You're proof of that."

"Yeah, you're right." Mike sighed through his nose, the anger seemingly draining from him in the face of Al's frustrated insistence. "And I *do* thank God every morning I wake up and there ain't bars on the windows. And every night, I go home and I give Chelsea a kiss and Lee a big hug and I thank Him up above again for giving me another chance."

It wasn't God who gave you that chance, Al wanted to say.

"Jesus." Mike's rag swept across the scarred, but otherwise immaculate, surface of the bar again as he scooped microscopic or imaginary particles from it into his open palm. "To think I missed most of the first four years of that boy's life. You know, she wasn't even gonna tell me he was mine? She didn't want him knowing his father was an ex-con. Never mind. I don't want to get into that. Don't know why I brought it up." He shook his head sadly. "I guess the point is that, in the end, everything's worked out okay for me. *But*," he looked his cousin straight in the eye, "that's *me*, Al. If you're serious about this, you gotta find your own way out."

"Yeah," Al said slowly, glumly.

Christ, the guy looks like he's gonna cry, Mike thought. His heart reached out to his cousin, but his hands kept the cleaning-rag moving.

"I feel like I'm drowning, Mike," Al began again. "I gotta get out. I can't do this shit no more." His voice cracked the slightest bit, just enough that he couldn't hide it. But he didn't stop. He couldn't. "Mike, they got me mowin' down teenagers like dogs in the street and they want me to beat on little old men for money they ain't got. And God fuckin' help me, I *do* it." His voice broke and he felt the tears starting to flow, but he didn't care. "What the hell kinda life is that?"

He leaned his head down, resting it on his forearms, crossed in front of him on the bar. He took a moment to compose himself, then turned enough so that his voice wouldn't be muffled. "And now… now they stuck me with this psycho kid. He's dumb as hell and violent as shit. Thinks it's all some fun, crazy game."

Don't let this *life be* your *life.* The words rattled around Al's head as beer sloshed around in his otherwise-empty stomach.

Al raised his head. "I guess I will have that shot, after all."

"You got it." Mike reached for a clean shot-glass for Al, glad for a distraction, for the change of subject. Before he could pour, though, the sound of sirens—both the long, whining call of firetrucks and the short, urgent one of police cars—barreling past the bar's open door caught both men's attention. None of the barflies seemed to take the least notice.

Mike came out from behind the bar, went to the front door, reaching it as a white and red SUV with a crown of flashing lights and red and gold livery that read "FIRE CHIEF" roared past. Only a second or two later, the deep-throated, squawking honk of another firetruck preceded the arrival of the vehicle itself, racing by at top speed. A police cruiser, blue lights flashing, followed practically on its bumper.

Al, having moved up behind Mike, leaned past his friend to stick his head out of the doorframe, face turned in the direction the vehicles were headed. Thick, black, angry-looking coils of smoke rose from behind the row of buildings a couple of blocks over.

"Shit, that's right around the corner."

***

Seated at the messy desk in the tiny backroom of the bodega, Nicole Edwards stared at the dusty computer monitor and sighed as she watched yet another ordinary-looking customer buy yet another coffee on the shop's security-recording. This one at least was wearing a suit, unlike the rest who had mostly been in casual wear.

And, she thought, *this one bought a newspaper, too. Variety really is the spice of life.*

The exterior video feed hadn't caught shit, exactly as Edwards predicted. It was instantly clear when they first saw the video that it didn't have a decent angle on or enough resolution to see the location of the shootings.

Edwards wanted to pack it in right there. The owner of the store had made them get a warrant before he'd allowed them access to his video and that cost them time they didn't really have. She was ready to try something else. But Park objected, as usual.

"Let's check the inside feed, too," he suggested.

"For what?" She couldn't see any possible sense in that. Nicole Edwards wasn't a lazy cop, but she wasn't one for chasing down astronomically-improbable potential leads, either. She liked to think of herself as pragmatic, and pragmatism meant not wasting time, as far as she was concerned.

Park threw her that goofy little grin she both hated and thought was sort of cute. Not that she thought of Park that way, but she was still a woman and she appreciated a good smile on a guy. "No place else around here to get a cup of coffee, right?" he said. "And even killers like their java. Who knows? We might get lucky and recognize someone."

Edwards glared at him, unamused, but finally assented – as usual.

The two of them went through footage from roughly four a.m. when the bodega opened until noon, just to be safe. They saw nothing of value, but over an hour in the poorly lit room with barely a need to focus on what was in front of her had gotten the wheels in Edwards's head moving. She had been a cop for more than a dozen years and a detective for almost half of that time. She was aware whose territory this area was and she knew exactly who the previous victims of those similar crimes were associated with.

Now, while Park was asking the owner of the shop a few questions about the neighborhood, Edwards was reviewing specific areas of the footage, reexamining certain individuals she'd seen to make sure none were familiar.

Unfortunately, predictably, none were.

She clicked the black X atop the computer window's right corner, sending the split-screen security footage back to the depths of the ancient PC's hard-drive. The desktop icon marked "SECURE-WATCH" remained highlighted as she turned towards her partner, now re-entering the cramped backroom with the store's nervous, impatient-looking owner – a wiry Indian man whose appearance reminded Edwards of the messy office he kept.

"I told you this would be a waste of time."

Park shrugged. "Hey, you never can tell. Something might still come of it."

"This means you're done? You'll be leaving?" the shopkeeper asked. "I need this room for business."

Edwards gave him a cool look before shifting her gaze and addressing her partner again. "Right. I'd like a copy of this for the tech guys to go over just in case."

Park turned towards the bodega's owner. "Is that okay, Mister Das?"

"Sure, sure. I always help if I can."

But not without a God-damned warrant, right? Some help. Edwards kept the thought to herself as she rose from the desk-chair.

"Great, we appreciate it. Thanks again for all your cooperation, Mister Das. If you could burn that onto a CD for me?" Park smiled at the other man as Edwards pushed past him, back out into the store, heading towards the street.

Outside, a few minutes later, Park joined her, stuffing a CD-R into an evidence envelope. Edwards looked at him askance and asked, "What was that bull about 'cooperation?' We had to wait almost an hour for the warrant that little shithead made us get to look at his worthless security footage." Angrily, she added, "I've got half a mind to toss that place. If he has nothing to hide, why bust our balls over the video?"

Park made a sort of facial shrug. "It's his right and we *were* intruding. Just because someone wants to make us follow the rules a little doesn't mean he isn't cooperating. Besides, I don't think thanking him hurts anything. Politeness is never wasted and maybe he'll remember it the next time someone needs a favor. Think of it as planting a seed." He gave her another goofy grin.

Edwards shook her head and got into the car which she'd moved to a spot near the bodega during their wait for the warrant. The radio blared to life the instant she placed the key in the ignition.

"All units, 10-72: fire in progress at 4333 West Storace Street. F.D. is on the scene and requests police back-up for crowd control."

"That's only a few blocks from here."

"Forget it, Jeff. They want unis, not detectives."

Park twisted in his seat to look at his partner. "Listen. This area has been primarily Italian for decades, but Hispanic gangs have been moving into the territory the last few years. You know, like —"

"Like our stiffs." Detective Edwards rolled her eyes. "I know very well who runs these neighborhoods. Or used to, anyway. The grip's slipping from what I've heard. But what's that got to do with a fire? What crazy conclusions are you jumping to in that shiny little head of yours?"

A slow half-smile appeared on Jeff Park's face as he ran a hand over his bald, but stubbly, head. "I'm not jumping to anything. But if they need us, they need us and I'm of the opinion that if you go where you're needed in life, you'll end up where you want to be."

Such hippy bullshit, Edwards thought, as she turned the engine over and shifted the car into gear.

But what the hell. It's not like there was anything better to do at the moment.

12

Jenna Ford's spike heels stabbed into the thin, dirty carpet of Bottoms Up as she strode through the murky interior, unconsciously swinging her rear in time to the throbbing jock-rock spewing from the overhead loudspeakers with every step she took. Topless, bottomless, or fully nude, Jenna was a dancer and some things were ingrained.

At a little past two o'clock, she practically had the place to herself aside from Phil, the daytime bartender, the listlessly swaying Latina girl with pert, cupcake breasts up on the stage and half a dozen patrons—mostly old men—scattered throughout the room. Only a few of the customers even seemed to be paying attention to the girl, whom Jenna didn't recognize, as she did a tired bump and grind routine that didn't seem the least bit sexy to Jenna. With this "crowd," though, it probably didn't matter one way or the other. Weekday afternoons were deathly slow at the best of times; Jenna was glad she'd graduated to "prime" dancing slots last year. Even sharing her apartment with two other women, she'd never make rent on what that poor girl up on stage would probably take home for the day.

Jenna's own stage-time was still hours in the future, but she often came in early, if only to be doing something aside from sitting around the house. And this early in the day, she was free to use the front entrance of the club instead of the door reserved for staff and performers, located around the back of the building. She liked to check out who was on stage – not because she thought of the other girls as competition, but because she was always on the lookout for new moves she might incorporate into her own act. "Stealing" dance moves was generally frowned on, but the turnover was so high in places like this that nobody noticed or cared, even if they did. Having spent three years at Bottoms Up, Jenna was basically a fixture and she spent more time in the club than she did at home.

She spent as little time at home as possible lately, in fact. She liked the girls she lived with, Wendy and Trish, but even with her own bedroom, the apartment often felt too small. All three were dancers, but Jenna was the only one who did it full-time. Her roommates did what they could to get by, including things Jenna thanked God she'd never found herself having to do. When one of her friends brought home tricks, every sound bounced around the place's few rooms, setting her skin crawling and her nerves on edge. Jenna didn't blame anyone for doing anything they had to in order to make ends meet, but that didn't mean she had to subject herself to it. She got plenty of cringe at work.

Tossing a little wave and a "hi" to Phil as she passed, Jenna entered the hallway leading towards the private areas of the building, past the half-dozen or so curtained alcoves that served as private-dance booths, through the hallway to where the individual dressing-rooms—one each for the four girls, including Jenna herself, who Denny, the club manager, rated "stars"—were located.

She entered her room, tossed her purse down onto the worn-out easy-chair near the window and settled onto the stool before the makeup table. She flicked on the mirror's built-in halo of lights and sighed at what she saw in its reflection.

She was tired. She looked it. Dark crescent-shaped smudges beneath her eyes, little crinkles in the corners. There was a slightly pasty quality to her complexion from too much night-work. She was glad she didn't have to dance during the day, but staying up all hours took its toll. The thought of a straight job never occurred to her, though. She was too far beyond that already.

Jenna stood and stretched like a cat, drawing each muscle in her body out to its full length, relishing the sensation as vertebrae in her neck and lower back popped. She flopped down onto the easy-chair, not even caring that her purse dug into her side, and rubbed her hands along its threadbare arms, remembering the previous night. She imagined her small, soft, pale hands were Al's big, scarred, rough ones. She could almost feel those powerful hands on the back of her head, toying with her hair as she moved up and down...

She wondered what he was doing at that very moment. She hated herself for it, thinking about how he had left things the night before. She had more self-respect than that, didn't she? She waved away the thought and tried to dismiss the emotion along with it.

This room was her place, her sanctuary. Sure, it was a dingy back room in a titty-club, but you take what you can get. Jenna wasn't proud and she was grateful for what she had. Grateful that Denny had given her a chance when she had literally nowhere else to go; grateful that she'd discovered in herself a talent at doing something marketable. There were people who had it a lot rougher than her. She knew that. She had a roof over her head and never went hungry. She never forgot to be grateful for those things.

And then there was Al. She was grateful to him, too, for seeing something in her – something he not only liked, but wanted to be near. Over the years at the club, thousands of guys had seen her dance. Many, hundreds probably, tried to talk to her, to pick her up. Only one had ever tried to get to know her first. Memories of those nights sent flutters through her belly.

She blew out a heavy breath and leaned deeper into the chair's fraying padding, her eyes fixed on the ceiling. On rare occasions when she was completely honest with herself, Jenna loved Al. Or at least thought she did. Some days she wasn't sure she understood exactly what "love" was. She'd dated plenty of men, but it was hard to fall in love with guys who saw you as nothing but a hole to fill.

Al wasn't like that.

Mostly.

Mostly he was good to her. And unlike Jenna's previous experiences with men, going back as far as she could remember — all the way back to her first boyfriend, Pete DeMamp, in sixth grade — it wasn't just about sex with Al. They talked, they laughed. He treated her like a person. For that, for his willingness to see beyond the surface of a tramped up little blonde whose bare tits were the first thing he'd noticed about her, she loved him – and she wanted to believe that at least some part of him loved her.

Only lately, it seemed less like he wanted to be near her and more like he wanted to *possess* her. Those suspicions had somehow tainted this place for Jenna. As ludicrous as it might have sounded to someone else, this club, this room in particular, always felt like a sort of home to her. But at the moment she didn't want to be anywhere near it. For the memories it contained, for the feelings it evoked and for the reminder that whatever she had imagined between them, Jenna was still just Al's side-piece.

Damn it, you son of a bitch, she thought as her eyes began to burn and she felt the tears start to well up. She pressed the palms of her hands against her eyes, willing herself to let it go – for the moment, at least.

Knock knock knock sounded at the door, twisting Jenna's head in that direction. She was surprised. Not many people knew she came in this early and the door had no lock, only a chain that had to be fastened from the inside. If one of the other girls wanted to borrow some makeup or something, they'd probably have just come in and taken it, then told her later on. Who knew she'd be in here and cared enough to knock? Phil, maybe?

Jenna stood. "Yeah?"

No answer.

Something stirred in her chest. Something she couldn't quite name, but didn't care for. Not fear, exactly, but something that put her senses on alert all the same.

She moved halfway across the room. "Phil?" she called, hesitantly.

Nothing.

Jenna crossed to the door, eyes skittering across the dingy surface towards the chain she hadn't bothered to fasten. Her heart began to race.

An image of Al, the last person to knock on that door, flashed through her brain. Hope as she might, she knew it wasn't Al, come to apologize for how he treated her the last time they saw each other.

She crossed the final few feet to the door and reached for the chain – just as the thin, hollow-core door flew open with a crash.

13

Al dashed a block and a half down East Street before realizing he was drawing as many stares as the emergency vehicles. The neighborhood was generally quiet unless disaster of some sort struck, but the inhabitants weren't fools: gunshots meant danger, but firetrucks meant excitement. People—mostly older folks, housewives and the perpetually out of work—were leaving their buildings, heading in the direction of the smoke to get a glimpse for themselves. Small groups moved together, talking in animated murmurs as something like a carnival atmosphere began to take shape. This was the most exciting thing that would happen to most of these folks all week.

The excitement these people felt, though, paled in comparison to the sense of urgency Al radiated. Racing through the sparse, but growing crowd, he was conspicuous. Everyone wanted to see what was going on, sure, but what was the hurry?

Al stopped, hunched forward to lean against a blue, steel mailbox and took deep, gulping breathes. He wasn't used to running, but he'd forced himself. He had a very bad feeling and it was growing worse.

Right before the corner of East Street and Benson Ave, he ducked into an alley, taking a shortcut to Storace Street – the same route he'd taken on his way to Mike's place.

As he'd raced out of the bar, his cousin called after him, "Hey! Al! Where the fuck you goin'?" confusion in his voice.

Al told Mike a lot, much more than he intended, but he hadn't said where he'd been prior to showing up at the bar – or what he'd been doing. It was better this way. Better, if it came to it, that Mike didn't know rather than being forced to a lie or, worse, to tell the truth.

Al saw them before he reached the end of the alley: a small gaggle of rubberneckers, congregating on the sidewalk between a busted-up looking Chevy Impala pulled halfway up onto the sidewalk—moving out of the way of the emergency vehicles, he guessed—and the buildings themselves, clogging the end of the alleyway.

Shit, he thought, once more slowing his hurried rush to a slow jog, to the pace of a man who wants to see what the excitement is about, not one who has a stake in it. Elbowing his way through the dozen or so people—mostly women, only a couple of older men thrown into the mix—saying, "Excuse me," loudly and repeatedly while muttering curses under his breath, he forced a path through the group. With his view of the scene down the block now unobstructed, his jog became a full-out run.

Even from a block up and across the street, it was clear that the building engulfed in flames was Magini's. Thick gouts of black, oily smoke poured from heat-ruptured windows, obscuring the upper floors of the building and casting a shadow across the sidewalk like a passing cloud obscuring the sun. Only this cloud was more than just a momentary intrusion.

The street was choked with people and vehicles, both emergency units and civilian vehicles caught up in the blockade that the police and fire departments hastily threw up to cordon off the area. Firefighters were working in three clearly coordinated teams, overseen from a makeshift command station set up out of the back of the SUV Al had seen earlier, the one marked "FIRE CHIEF." Under their leader's direction, two teams hosed down the buildings on either side of Magini's Drugs, keeping the fire from spreading. A third team battled the blaze itself, red, flickering flames reflecting off of their helmets and faceplates, making them appear to be bathed in a sort of sunset glow. Even at a distance, Al could feel the heat on his upturned face. Inside the building, it must have been like a portal to hell.

An ambulance, lights flashing but siren silent, waited in the middle of the street, not far from where Al emerged from the crowd. By the vehicle's rear bumper, emergency medical technicians stood at the ready, watching for burn or smoke-inhalation victims, ready to provide whatever assistance the firefighters might need.

A pair of police cruisers blocked off the street on either side of Magini's, four officers attempting to hold back a crowd of what must have been more than a hundred people, split into two groups gathered on either end of the block. Where the crowd was thickest, at the edge of the police's hastily thrown-up barrier, Al was forced to stop. He scanned the scene, for a split second catching the eye of a uniformed cop trying to calm the press of spectators, before turning away. Al's heart thumped in his chest; the smart thing was to walk away. Right now, this very instant. Just go back to where he'd parked the car, climb inside and drive away. But he couldn't. He had to know for sure.

Al turned, head swiveling, eyes searching and finally, there he was. On the fringe of the crowd, still in his white shirt, bowtie and druggist's apron, stood Stuart Magini, looking small and alone, eyes glassy as they stared up at the raging inferno that had been both his business and his home.

"Mister Magini! Jesus Christ in Heaven!" Al crossed the distance separating them, using one elbow to bull his way through the crowd, his other arm outstretched toward the older man as if to pull him closer.

Magini's head jerked, as if startled from sleep, then turned toward the sound of Al's voice. The look of misery-steeped wonder on his face twisted into a mask of cold rage.

Al's hands fell on the smaller man's shoulders. He pulled Magini aside, out of the group he'd stood with, across the street and into the shadow of a building well away from the fire and the crowd and its sea of ears. The old man gave no resistance, allowing himself to be led away like a docile child.

Must be in shock, Al realized.

Keeping Magini at arm's length, Al looked him over, scanning for obvious damage. "Mister Magini, you okay?"

Al looked away, towards where the blaze raged, and shook his head. Half-whispering, he said, "Christ, what a fucking mess."

Magini said nothing. The anger that burned in his eyes, every bit the equal of the blaze consuming his store, made it unnecessary.

One hand still around Magini's upper arm, Al leaned in, pressed his mouth close to the old man's ear. "I swear to you, I didn't do this. This is not how Mister Castella does business."

The old man stiffened, but, suddenly conscious of the pressure Al exerted on his arm, of the other man's proximity, of the weight of Al's presence, he maintained his silence.

Somehow, that was worse than anything Al that could imagine him saying.

His tone softer, Al added, "Mister Magini, you *know* me."

The fire in the druggist's eyes cooled slightly. He closed them, shook his head slowly, sadly. "I know you wouldn't do this. At least, I want to *hope* that you wouldn't, Al, but that boy you had with you… Benny, you called him."

"That son of a fuckin' bitch," Al swore, his fist balling of its own accord, raised and poised to smack into the brick of the nearby building. He told Magini this wasn't how Castella did business, but suddenly, it felt like a lie.

"Hey, folks, let's move up the street a bit more, huh?" As one, Al and Magini turned toward the sound of the new voice. A shaven-headed Asian man in a rumpled, navy-blue suit approached, gesturing with two fingers as if he could push the other men along with the power of suggestion.

The man turned, made a sweeping movement with his arms to encompass a few other, scattered people hovering around the edge of the crowd, between the main body of onlookers and where Al and Magini stood. As he did so, the jacket of his suit rose slightly and Al noticed the holstered nine-millimeter pistol riding one hip and the gold shield pinned to his belt above the other.

Raising his voice, the cop added, "I know things like this can be interesting, exciting even, but having bystanders crowding around makes it all the more difficult and dangerous for folks to do their jobs."

Magini and Al shared a look. It didn't escape Detective Park's attention.

"Everything okay, fellas? You hear what I said? Let's give the firefighters some room to do their jobs."

"That's my store," Magini said, a finger raised in the direction of the blaze.

Park didn't miss a beat. He cast a glance at Al, one eyebrow raised. Then, to Magini, he said, "Are you the Magini in 'Magini's Drugs?'" Without waiting for an answer, the detective continued, "Okay, well, still, let's get out of everybody's way. Why don't you come with me, for now? I want to get you looked at by the EMTs. Were you in the building when the fire broke out?"

The wave of words washed over Magini, seemingly with no effect. The old man had shut down again, staring at the flaming building as if hypnotized.

"Mister Magini?"

No response.

Park turned his attention towards Al, scrutinizing him, as if only now really seeing him for the first time.

"You a friend of Mister Magini's?"

"No. I'm—" Al's cellphone chose that moment to go off, the muted buzzing he'd set for his text-alerts saving him from having to lie to someone trained to detect such things. "Excuse me," he said, holding up a finger and turning away.

He reached into his jacket pocket, pulled out the buzzing black box, and flipped it open. "Jenna" the "sender" field read.

Christ, what's she want now? Al wondered, irritated. A clingy side-piece was the last thing he wanted to deal with at the moment, though he was glad for the distraction, for the chance to turn from the cop without having to make up some excuse.

He opened the message and read: "FUCK THIS BITCH AND FUCK YOU TOO."

"What the fuck?" he blurted.

***

Park guided the unresisting Magini toward where an ambulance was parked, putting a hand on the shoulder of the man Magini had been speaking with as they passed. "Sir, why don't you accompany your friend here while we get him checked out?"

The beefy, graying man in the expensive, but worn, charcoal suit spun on his heel, brushing Park's hand away from him. Glowering, he growled, "Buzz off," before stomping away towards the mouth of an alley, fingers stabbing angrily at the keys of his old-fashioned flip-phone.

Park shook his head, but let him go. Being an asshole wasn't illegal.

To his charge, he said, "C'mon, Mister Magini, I really want to get you checked out, then we can—"

"Park, what's up?"

Nicole Edwards strode towards them, emerging from the mass of the crowd with a look of vaguely annoyed concern on her face.

***

"It's Jenna. You know the drill." A drawn-out *beep* followed the short voicemail greeting.

119

"Shit," Al muttered. Then louder, "Shit! This is all I fuckin' need." He snapped the phone shut, shoved it hard into the outer pocket of his suit-jacket. He glanced around, realizing he'd drawn stares from the cop wrangling Magini, and then turned away, heading in the direction of the spot where he'd parked the Crown Vic on the far side of Storace. He moved quickly past Magini, the concerned-looking Asian cop, and the woman who'd joined them, purposely ignoring all three.

He managed a dozen steps before a husky female voice called out from somewhere behind him: "Hey, hold up a second."

***

Moments earlier, Nicole Edwards had spotted her partner through the crowd, speaking with a pair of men: one somewhere in his late forties and another who was in that nebulous range between mid-sixties and early seventies. The older of the two men wore a white apron and had an air of confusion about him. The other radiated an intensity that made her instantly wary.

Edwards walked towards the small group, the edges of the crowd of onlookers parting around her like she was the wind moving through tall grass; something about the way she moved said in no uncertain terms that it was best to be where she wasn't.

She saw Jeff Park steer the man in the apron away from where they were standing, while pointing towards the waiting ambulance and its cadre of EMTs. He said something to the third man, put a hand on his shoulder. The guy twisted away from Park's touch, said something she didn't quite catch over the clamor of the commotion around her. The man stalked away, cellphone in hand.

Though still a dozen feet away, Edwards called towards Park.

"This is Mister Magini, the owner of the drugstore," Park told her. "And that's his friend, I guess?" He made it a question, looking towards Magini for confirmation, but received only a vacant look from the old man. Park shrugged. "Well, either way, I want to get Mister Magini—"

"Shit!" the guy with the phone shouted, loud enough to interrupt Park's train of thought.

***

"Fuck," Al spat. "I ain't got time for this."

It was the worst thing to do, the thing that could only raise more questions, do nothing but make these cops take an interest in him. He did it, anyway.

Al ran.

He thought he'd been running before, on his way to discover the source of the blaze, to confirm his fears, but now he charged down the street as if his life depended on it. Maybe his didn't, but he was pretty sure that Jenna's did.

"Stop! Police!" The cry from behind him competed with the roar of the fire and the chaos of everything going on around it, but was still clear enough.

Al ignored it. All he could think of was to keep moving.

***

I've seen that guy, Edwards thought when she was close enough to get a good look. The bodega's video footage, she realized. She didn't believe in coincidences.

"Hey! Hold up a second," she called towards him. Too late. He snapped his phone shut and took off like a shot.

She gave chase.

"Stop! Police!" she shouted. It was futile, but without identifying herself as a cop, he could reasonably claim later on that he was running in fear of the woman who suddenly charged after him.

Not that he had much to fear, she realized. The guy had a good head-start on her and as he disappeared around a corner, down a narrow side-street, she realized that even without it, she probably wouldn't have been able to catch up to him. *"Impressive speed for a guy his age,"* she would later admit.

Detective Edwards was breathing hard when the stitch in her side struck her like a kidney-punch, but she didn't stop. She was close, almost to the mouth of the street the man disappeared down.

But not close enough.

Before she made it to the corner of the alley, a vehicle roared out of it, taking the turn with a high-pitched screech of rubber on blacktop and the creak of straining steel. The gray Crown Victoria—nearly the same color as the man's suit, the observer in her noted—sped up as soon as it hit the straightaway, blowing through a stop sign and disappearing into the distance within moments.

But not before she noted something else: the license plate.

14

Lexi Vacarro flicked a strand of still naturally blonde hair away from her face with an irritated brush of her hand, finished folding the bath towel before her then tossed it casually towards the laundry basket, where it flopped on top of a pile of its kin.

She let out a sigh, glancing towards the clock on the living room wall. Ten after three in the afternoon. The kids had just gotten home from school and it was time to start thinking about what to make for dinner, but there was still a mountain of laundry to do, plus the vacuuming she'd been putting off since yesterday morning.

Lexi's thoughts drifted towards the previous night, to the conversation Al refused to have with her. *"I can't keep raising these kids alone, Al,"* she'd sobbed, giving in for a moment to the despair she fought against daily. She recognized that now, that this dull ache somewhere in the pit of her being was despair. Nothing soothed it, nothing could even touch it. All she could do was try to push it away, but it was always there, always waiting to surge back up. It took a lot to even acknowledge that fact, to put a name to it, even privately. Last night was the closest she'd ever come to admitting it to someone else.

And at the last instant, she chickened out, backed off, when Al—quite effectively—had shut her down.

But the worst part of it? Somehow, she felt guilty. *She* felt guilty. And that both disgusted her and made that sinking feeling all the deeper.

From the outside, her life didn't seem that bad. She had a nice home; she had two great kids; she never had to worry about where the next meal was coming from. There was even the beginning of college funds for both Beth and Kyle sitting in the bank. Many people—so, so many—had things much worse than she did. So what if her husband worked all hours? Lots of people's spouses did. It was all for her and the kids, wasn't it?

Except it wasn't. Not all of it. She knew that; Lexi wasn't stupid.

Sure, Al worked a lot. He spent long hours at the shipping company's offices and he had important responsibilities that kept him busy, that made him integral to the company's operations. She'd been to the Christmas parties, she'd talked to his coworkers. They spoke highly of him. And before they were married, she worked the phones at a similar operation – she knew the kinds of crazy schedules multiple warehouses with trucks coming in and out, day and night, forced a business to operate on.

But trucking warehouses didn't make you come home smelling of perfume, cigarettes, and a certain, distinctive musk. Al tried to hide it, in a half-assed sort of way, by coming home late, when he could reasonably expect the household to be asleep. She almost appreciated that, in a way. At least he wasn't throwing it in her face. And the kids didn't have a clue; she was grateful for that much. But Lexi wasn't as heavy a sleeper as Al believed her to be and her sense of smell worked fine, even in a darkened bedroom.

If it only happened once, she might have been able to quietly forgive and try to force herself to forget. Just one more thing to push down and hide and try to ignore. When it happened a second time, she let the anger grow. The tenth time, she decided she'd start greeting Al when he came home, no matter how late it was. And she'd done exactly that for almost a year now. But even so, she'd never yet gotten up the nerve to confront him. Instead, the best she could manage was passive-aggressiveness and crying jags.

For that, Lexi hated herself. Hated the weakness, the lack of resolve. Wherever Al was going, whatever he was doing — and with whom, she only occasionally allowed herself to add — Al was her husband; they made a promise to each other. She had every right to be furious, to nurture this thing inside of her that burned to be unleashed.

But for all that, she couldn't bring herself to hate *him*. Even with everything he put her through — not through malice, but merely neglect, she had to remind herself — she still saw love in his eyes when he was with the kids, and even sometimes when he looked at her. And when that happened, she saw in him the man she'd fallen in love with more two decades ago. She remembered how those pale-brown eyes of his carried something in them that she found almost mystically compelling – something she wanted to discover for herself. For a time, she thought she had. Maybe she did for a little while, before it slipped away again, out of her grasp and beneath the surface of the man he'd become. But it was still in there; she was sure of that, at least when she caught him looking at her the way he had so long ago.

"God damn it," she huffed softly, under her breath, resuming her folding, wanting to subsume the darkness in simple, rote domesticity for just a few minutes more. She glanced at the wall-clock again: almost three-thirty now. She was shocked; she'd let herself wallow in those thoughts for close to twenty minutes.

Time flies... flashed through her brain, but the crashing sound from directly above her head interrupted the thought.

"Kids? What are you up to?" she called towards the ceiling, standing up from the couch.

The only response was muted giggling and the pitter-patter cadence of kid-sized feet running across the carpeted second floor.

Lexi closed her eyes, took a deep breath through her nose then called again towards the ceiling above her, "Beth! Kyle! Keep it to a dull roar up there. I'm serious, guys! No craziness today, okay?"

Lexi looked at the pile of half-folded laundry before her, listening to the muffled sounds of the kids playing upstairs. From outside the house, she heard the ordinary noise of light traffic, of birdsong, of a dog barking somewhere down the street. A peaceful soundtrack for the suburbs. The phone picked that moment to go off, the shrill electronic noise making her jump. She snatched the receiver from the end-table next to the sofa, paused, and then, without bothering to look at the caller ID, replaced it in its cradle, disconnecting the call.

Lexi sighed heavily, sat back down on the couch, put her head in her hands and began to cry.

126

15

Al yanked the steering wheel to the left, swerving into the oncoming lane to pass a slow-moving panel-truck whose indecisive driver had flicked on his right turn-signal close to a mile ago. The Crown Victoria's big engine roared as he put on speed to pass, surging up to nearly sixty miles an hour in an instant—twenty-five over the speed-limit—then swinging back into his own lane, barely missing a head-on collision with a station-wagon whose driver looked both furious and terrified. The woman flipped Al the bird. He ignored her. On any other day, he would have at least reciprocated. On any other day, he wouldn't have been driving like a maniac.

Al's eyes slid across the screen of his cellphone again, wedged upright in the nearest cup-holder beneath the dash, hoping to see he'd missed a call, had received a text... any sign of response from Jenna. After he'd made it to the car, back on Storace Street, and pointed the vehicle in the direction of Bottoms Up—all the way across town from Magini's Drugs—he'd allowed himself a moment to catch his breath then tried calling the girl again. There was no response save her voicemail's greeting. He tried sending a text, but it sat in the digital ether, showing a status of sent, as yet unread. He called twice more before giving up to focus on the road. Jenna didn't dance afternoons and her phone rarely left her hand when she wasn't working, but that text obviously hadn't come from her. The possibility of someone getting hold of her phone and sending it as a bad joke wasn't nil, but it also wasn't likely. The most likely possibility scared him shitless.

Al refocused with a short, sharp shake of his head, snapping himself back to the moment. He turned the steering wheel right, pulling the car onto Walthrop Drive. The light industrial district near the western edge of town gave way to a long strip of fast-food restaurants, gas-stations, and convenience stores. The heavier traffic generated by all those high-turnover businesses slowed his progress, adding to his anxiety.

Al grit his teeth in frustration as a rusted-out hatchback swerved in front of him, cutting him off, only to proceed at half the speed-limit.

"C'mon, you stupid motherfucker. Get the lead out," he cursed under his breath.

On a good day, when he hit the green lights right and traffic wasn't too heavy, Bottoms Up, near the corner of Somerset and Walthrop, was twenty-five minutes across the city from where Al had started, on the east side by the river. On a bad day, like today, when everyone was dragging ass and every light seemed to take twice as long as usual, it might take as many as forty minutes. But, driving like a mad man, ignoring stop signs, passing other cars in increasingly dangerous ways, Al made it in a little over fifteen.

The Crown Vic pulled into the club's parking lot, crunching over the bump where the cracked blacktop met the sidewalk, jostling Al in his seat. He slid the vehicle into a space by the front of the building, hopped out, slamming the car's door behind him harder than he intended. He crossed the short distance to the entrance, one hand unconsciously moving to the holstered weapon beneath his left shoulder. He had no idea of what awaited him inside the club – only fear of what he'd find.

The steel-and-glass door swung open easily, and the beaded inner curtain parted with his passage, but the third "door" stepped up to block Al's entrance into the club proper.

"Yo, not so fast. See the sign? We got a cover here." A huge hand fell just short of Al's chest.

In the dim light of the place, the new bouncer's size and "SECURITY"-emblazoned t-shirt made him more recognizable than his face – bearded and seeming perpetually bored. The other man's eyes were apparently sharper than Al's, or at least better-accustomed to the low light, as recognition flashed across his expression.

"Oh, hey. Wassup, man? Back so soon?" The guy tried to make the greeting sound friendly. On another day, Al would have appreciated the gesture. Today, he didn't give a rat's ass.

"Get the fuck outta my way." He brushed roughly past the larger man, nearly shoving him aside in his haste, concern, and annoyance. Only a hint of surprise showed through the bouncer's professional mask. Despite his fear and anxiety, part of Al was still impressed; the guy was well-suited to this line of work and could sense when not to push. A place like this needed a cool head working the door. He'd probably have a job here as long as he wanted it.

Al crossed the club's nearly empty main room through an aural haze of bass-heavy hip-hop, heedless of the girl on stage, down on her belly, dry-humping the polished wooden floor. Her glittery thong and oil-drenched body flashed and sparkled as it caught the light with the movement of her grinding hips. The stage's mirrored backdrop made it appear as if a small army of identical girls were doing a choreographed routine. The effect was lost on Al. So close to his goal, his focus was razor-sharp.

Through the door marked "PRIVATE," Al hurried towards the four dressing rooms in the deepest recesses of the building, icy tendrils crawling through his guts. At this time of day, the place was as quiet as it ever got, but the relative silence was worrying rather than comforting. Nobody around meant no witnesses, which meant more chances for...
It didn't bear thinking about.

Al's knuckles wrapped sharply once, twice on Jenna's door. "Jenna! You in there?"

He waited half a moment before pushing the door open.

His face twisted in horror at the scene before him, his fears realized. He rushed in, falling to his knees beside the girl, crumpled on the floor. "Jesus, Mary, and Joseph!"

Jenna lay in the middle of the room, semiconscious, her face and exposed chest a map of black and blue, accented in red. Blood seeped from a gash somewhere on her scalp, dyeing her bottle-blonde hair a darker color. Her lips were a mashed-up mess; it looked as if one of her teeth had been pushed clean through her lower lip. Her right eye was swollen almost completely shut and, to Al's experienced eye, the socket looked broken.

Slowly, gently, Al pulled the woman's head into his lap, one arm supporting her around the shoulders, tugging the remains of her top up to preserve a measure of her dignity. "Baby," he said softly. "What happened? Who *did* this?"

The sound of the familiar voice brought Jenna closer to the surface. Struggling through a fog of darkness and pain, frustrated with the way her body and brain seemed to refuse her commands, all she could manage was a single, croaked word: "Al?"

"Oh, Jesus. Jesus..." Al closed his eyes, took a deep breath. "Jenna, baby... what happened?" He already knew the answer, but he needed to hear it.

Jenna swallowed, her abused body fighting even so simple an action. Her tongue probed her mouth, running along the edge of a broken tooth. The sharpness of the pain brought everything into focus.

"I knew," she began, so quietly Al was forced to lean in close to hear her, his ear only inches from her mouth. "That you'd...come. Even if...you nuh..." The sound became a groan. She sucked in a short, rattling breath and tried again. "Never stay long. I knew you'd.... come. You always," she interrupted herself again, the words becoming a ragged gasp. Finally, slowly, she said, "You always make time for me."

The dig struck Al like a blow. This was his fault; he didn't need to be told that. And it was obvious who did this, but he needed to hear Jenna say the name. The guilt was already overwhelming, but the waiting was agony.

"Baby, please," Al prompted. "I know it hurts… but tell me who did this to you. *Please*."

Jenna's uninjured eye fluttered, her throat pulsed with the effort of swallowing. Then, as if she hadn't heard Al, she continued, her voice a little stronger, as if the talking helped, as though she was simply out of practice. "He knew you'd come, too. T-took my phone and said you'd come. Said when you did, to tell you, 'This is what you get… f-for making me look like a bitch.'"

Al's heart hammered in his chest and his stomach churned, the bile creeping up his esophagus like the deep, dark rage that threatened to explode from the core of his being. It was Benny. Al didn't have the slightest shred of doubt, but unless she said the name…

He couldn't even say why it mattered. But it did.

"Jenna… just say the name. Tell me who did this. One word's all I need." His voice was cold, flat, tightly controlled.

The answer was a whisper: "Benny."

Even knowing it, Al somehow wasn't prepared. His body shook with anger, his vision blurred. "Jenna, I'm so sorry."

In Al's arms, the injured woman struggled to sit up straighter, to look him in the eye with her own, at least the one not swollen shut. "He said, too… to tell you, 'You make me look like a bitch, I make your bitches pay.'"

"Hey, everythin' okay in here? One of the girls said she heard yellin' a minute ago and — oh, shit."

Teeth bared in a snarl, Al's head whipped towards the voice coming from the doorway. The bouncer stood outside the doorway, his professional mask fallen away, an expression of shock and horror in its place.

The two men's eyes met. Something crackled in the air between them.

The bigger, younger man spoke first. "What the fuck, man? What the fuck did you —"

Gently as he could, Al lowered Jenna to the floor, then leapt to his feet, whirling on the bouncer, glad for a target he could take out a measure of his rage on. He grabbed the man's shirt in his fists, pulling him down to eye level, and growled, "Call fuckin' nine-one-one! Right now! And you God-damned well better stay with her until they get here. Keep her safe or I'll have your fuckin' balls, I swear to Christ. Anyone but you or an EMT sets foot in this room, I'll do to you what he did to her, you understand me?"

Al released the man, pushing him away with enough force that the larger man's shoulder careened off of the doorjamb as he backed away, stunned by the force of the rage on Al's face and in his voice. But he complied, drawing his cellphone from the pocket of his jeans as Al knelt down next to Jenna again, pressing a gentle kiss to the woman's forehead.

"I gotta go, baby. But I'll be back, I promise. I just gotta go make this right."

Through broken teeth and shredded lips, Jenna somehow managed a smile. "See… you never stay long."

The weight of those words cut Al deeply, but there was no time to dwell on it.

***

Outside, squinting against the brightness of the day, Al dialed Castella, his thumb flashing over the buttons of his cellphone with the speed of practiced repetition.

The connection didn't even get through a full ring before a deep voice answered, "Go ahead."

"Marty!" Al cried. "Let me talk to Mister Castella."

"Sorry, Al. I can't do that."

Al could picture Martin Teehan shaking his huge head back and forth slowly, a well-used gesture for the big man. As Castella's gatekeeper, he dealt with most of the little shit the boss himself didn't have time for or interest in.

"What? Why the fuck not?"

"This is about Benny, Al." It wasn't a question.

"Yeah! He's gone off the God-damned deep-end. He just kicked the living shit out of one of the girls at Bottoms Up and I'm pretty sure he set a fuckin' fire on the east side. I need—"

"You *need* to shut up a second," Teehan cut in. "Benny told Mister Castella all about your little tiff and how you been playing fast and loose with Castella's money lately."

"What?" Al gasped, shocked. "No, that's not—"

"Mister Castella is well aware that your revenues in certain areas are way down lately, Al, and he was wondering why. You been with us a long time and personally, I'd like to give you the benefit of the doubt on this one. Hell, on anything I didn't see you fucking up with my own two eyes, if I'm honest. I know you, Al, and if I were up to me, this situation would never even have arisen to begin with. We would have had a discussion and gotten some answers and everything would remain calm and peaceful and I wouldn't have to answer calls like this."

"Marty, let me talk to Mister Castella. Please."

Teehan ignored him. "But it isn't up to me," he continued, then paused. Al had a mental image of the other man shrugging massive shoulders, as Teehan added, "And we *are* having this call because the answer Benny has provided seems believable to Mister Castella. So... work it out between the two of you, Al—you and Benny—and if you can, then maybe Castella will have something to say about all of this."

Desperation clawed at Al. He couldn't believe what he was hearing. How the fuck could that God-damned kid turn Castella against him like that, with a snap of his fingers? Sure, they weren't as close as they used to be, but he'd been in this organization thirty fucking years. Didn't that count for anything?

"Marty, will you listen? I've worked for Castella, for *you*, longer than that fuckin' kid's been alive. I think I've earned—"

Teehan's sigh filled the line, drowning Al out. "Al, I don't make the rules or give the orders, I just follow 'em. Same as you. And you know as well as I do that seniority don't mean shit when it's an issue of trust. I'm sorry. I am. And like I said, if it was up to me..." He trailed off. A moment later, the connection broke.

"God damn it!" Al roared, slamming his fist down on the roof of the Crown Vic hard enough to dent it. "Fuck!" he screamed at the top of his lungs, drawing stares from a pair of passersby. He wasn't even aware of them.

Al unlocked the driver-side door and slid behind the wheel of the car. The engine came to life with the full-throated roar of a V8. He threw it in gear, backed out of his parking space fast enough to make the tires squeal and spit gravel, and then roared out into the street.

He flipped open his cellphone again, hit the first speed-dial entry. The connection rang once, connected, and then broke.

What the hell? He thought as he redialed. The connection rang again once, twice, three times, four times, a fifth time. Finally —

"... Hello?"

"Lexi?" A wave of relief washed over him. He didn't even notice the hoarseness of her voice. "Lexi, thank God!"

"Al? What's going on?"

"Listen, pack the kids up. I'm comin' home right now and we're gonna go upstate to your mother's or somewhere."

"What? Why?" Confusion, and a hint of fear, leapt into her voice.

Rage flared. Al snapped, "Because it's fuckin' important, that's why!" He took a shuddering breath, reigning the beast back in momentarily. Scaring Lexi wouldn't help a God-damned thing. Making her angry would be even worse, maybe make her ignore him altogether.

His tone softer, he said, "Please don't argue. Please just do as I ask." He took a short, shuddering breath, in and out, then added, "And, Lexi, baby, no matter what happens, I love you and the kids. Don't ever, ever forget that."

Without waiting for a response, Al snapped the phone shut, cutting off any reply.

16

The dead air of an abruptly ended connection roared in Lexi's ear for several moments before she came to herself enough to replace the cordless phone in its cradle. She looked around the living room in a daze, unsure of exactly what had happened. The familiar scene around her suddenly seemed somehow alien.

Al never called during the workday; not in years, anyway. When they were first married, he would call a couple of times throughout the day just to tell her how much he loved her, how much he missed her – and what he planned to do to her when he got home. She would blush and giggle out promises that she'd make good on when he returned home in the evenings. That newlywed behavior petered out, of course, as they settled into married life, but even after Beth was born, he'd call a few times a week, during his lunch break, to check in. By the time Kyle joined the family, those little calls were a thing of the past.

But it wasn't the call itself that shocked Lexi or that he'd said more to her in those few seconds on the phone than he had over the past week combined. The content was certainly disturbing and the amount of emotion with which Al had said it...

What could possibly be happening?

Lexi picked up the phone again, nearly hit redial to call him back. This was stupid, all this internal dissection of a simple phone call. Whatever was going on, either Al was overreacting or she was simply misinterpreting his intention.

But still…

A tremor ran through her, found its way to her stomach and set it to twisting in upon itself.

Something had been building for a long, long time. She took a hard look at her surroundings, at the home she and her husband had built. It hadn't felt right for a long time. A long, *long* time. It wasn't just the cheating or that he refused to talk to her about even critical things. There was something else, something entirely outside of whatever insight she had into her husband's life. Something he was dragging home with him that he couldn't quite shake.

The flash of intuition jolted her. Whatever was going on with Al, she told herself she was finally going to learn what it was, whether she really wanted to or not. And now, despite everything that came before, she was almost certain that she didn't really want to know.

Lexi turned, bare feet padding towards the front hallway then halfway up the stairs to the second floor.

"Kids?" she called. "Get your overnight bags out of the hall closet."

17

The Crown Victoria's engine roared as it barreled up the freeway on-ramp, barely squeezing past a pair of rice-burner motorcycles sitting at the top, waiting for a chance to ease into the tightly packed afternoon traffic. Al made his own chance. He put the gas-pedal to the floor, cutting off a dingy-green, rust-spotted Ford Explorer by the narrowest of margins, the sedan's rear end fishtailing slightly before regaining traction and leaping forward, putting a safe distance between Al's bumper and the SUV's grill.

In the rearview mirror, Al caught a flash of the other driver's furious face, eyes blazing and lips flapping—with obscenities, he was sure—before it faded away into the distance behind him. The other man's anger didn't bother him, nor did the thought of some nameless mook cursing him out, especially when he couldn't even hear it. There was jack-all the guy could do to him. No, what bothered him was the intrusion into someone else's life. That was something people would remember and Al had managed to live the life he had for three decades only because he took pains not to stand out. This insane driving was exactly the sort of thing that put you on people's radar. Today alone, he'd left more evidence of his existence in other people's minds than he probably had in the past six months.

But there was no helping it. He had already gotten on the wrong person's radar, under the wrong person's *skin*, and in doing so put other people's lives in danger. Lives he cared about. Al said a silent prayer, asking whatever angel or demon might be listening, *"Please, let me be wrong,"* though he knew in the pit of his stomach that he wasn't.

He pulled the steering wheel to the left and the Crown Vic slid into the passing lane to avoid rear-ending a bright-red convertible that appeared as if from nowhere.

Not nowhere. Al bit the inside of his cheek hard enough to break the skin and draw blood. The pain helped him focus on the moment he was in, to keep from drifting out again. "Wake the fuck up," he said out loud.

Eyes gliding across the speedometer, Al tapped the brakes, easing back from close to ninety miles an hour to a more sedate eighty – only fifteen miles above the posted limit. The big, gray four-door complied eagerly and Al was glad for the time he'd taken to find a Police Interceptor model at a used-car auction. The thing wasn't much to look at, but it handled like a dream. This was exactly the type of situation Al wanted it for while hoping that he'd never need to test the car's capabilities.

The space between Al and a seemingly meandering minivan, weaving slightly in the lane and going at least ten miles below the speed-limit, disappeared almost instantly. Al cut to the right, slammed the gas-pedal down. The big car leapt forward like a stone from a slingshot and cut through the space between the van's tail in the passing lane and the front end of a semi-tractor-trailer in the right lane. The semi's air-horn honked alarmingly close behind him. Al blocked it out, aware of the insane risks he was taking and not caring for a moment. All that mattered was reaching home. His foot pressed harder on the gas-pedal.

***

Warren Pettifer took a sip of the lukewarm coffee from the stainless steel mug he'd been nursing for going on four hours. He preferred his coffee hot, but while it had cooled considerably, the coffee, creamer, and sugar had settled into a pleasantly mellow mixture that he had to admit had its charms. Just below eye level and to the left of the steering wheel, numbers flashed crazily across the read-out of the window-mounted radar gun: sixty-six, sixty-eight, seventy. All over the posted sixty-five miles-per-hour limit. All beneath the point at which he could be bothered to pull anyone over.

The low whisper of his radio against the sounds of passing traffic formed a murmur of white noise that Pettifer found strangely lulling. He yawned, one half-closed eye drifting towards the dash-mounted clock. Three-forty in the afternoon. Two hours and twenty minutes until quitting time. Speed-trap duty was boring as hell, but he sort of liked the monotony. It could certainly be worse. Most days, he only issued a handful of tickets — six or seven most days, a dozen tops when it was really busy — and at twenty minutes or so per stop, that gave him plenty of time to himself. To think his own thoughts, to sneak a nap here and there. The sight of the patrol vehicle itself was enough to deter most speeders – at least within range of the radar gun. And outside of that range? Well, what he didn't know couldn't bother him.

Pettifer sighed, blinked his eyes rapidly, opened them as wide as he could a few times in what he called "visual flexing," and sighed. He picked up the coffee mug from its spot in the cup-holder, sloshed the liquid inside around and brought it towards his mouth again. The dashboard clock ticked silently up to three-forty-one.

A high-pitched, electronic whine cut through the calm stillness inside the car like a digital banshee. Pettifer sat up straight, choking on a swallow of coffee, some of it dribbling from between his lips to ooze down his chin as he struggled to regain his breath. His gaze flew to the radar-gun's display screen; angrily flashing red numbers read one-two-six.

"Holy shit!" he shouted, twisting in the driver's seat towards where a flash of gray had already screamed past him, immediately lost to sight.

Pettifer slammed the car into gear, in the same instant hitting both the light and sirens with a practiced flick of the wrist. Pulling out of the little, grass-lined dirt strip in the median between north- and south-bound lanes where he'd been parked, he put his foot to the gas-pedal. The crush of vehicles on the highway divided before him like Moses parting the Red Sea, as he chased after what, from the glimpse he'd gotten, looked like a car nearly identical to his own, save for a dull-gray primer color and lack of police livery.

The speeder had a good lead, but Pettifer wasn't about to let that discourage him. In eight years as a cop, and a tremendous number of hours spent sitting, waiting, in speed-traps, he had never seen anyone driving so fast. A drunk approaching a hundred, right in the middle of evening rush-hour, three or four years was ago was the highest he'd experienced; it was a miracle there'd been no accident. Even from a distance, though, as he began to close with the speeding vehicle, it was obvious this driver wasn't some lead-footed drunk. The way the gray sedan wove in and out of traffic, taking crazy risks but somehow making them work each time, was more than impressive – it was nearly mesmerizing. Whoever was behind that wheel was very, very skilled.

The now anything but bored cop palmed the handheld unit for the radio, depressing the send button with his grip. "This is unit forty-three, passing mile marker sixty-eight on highway two-thirty-one. I've got a speeder doing better'n a hundred-twenty and he's trying to get away from me."

The response was instantaneous. "Copy, forty-three. Make, model and plate?"

Pettifer squinted. The other vehicle's driver must have noticed him as the guy was now weaving even more frantically in and out of the lanes, trying to put vehicles between himself and his pursuer.

"Uh, gray, Ford Crown Victoria. Probably an Interceptor model the way this guy's handling it. Plate is..." He trailed off, futilely willing his eyesight to greater sharpness. "Damn it. I'm not sure," he said. "Starts with bravo, then there's a seven and a nine. That's all I can make out, dispatch."

"Copy, we'll put out the call."

Pettifer grit his teeth. Eight years he'd been waiting for something like this, for a chance to prove himself, for a story he could tell later. He wasn't going to blow it.

***

The red and blue lights grew bigger in Al's rearview, the siren fighting to make itself heard over the roar of the car's engine and the rushing of the wind that raced past with the speed of a tornado.

"God damn it, not now!" Al growled.

He pressed the pedal to the floor and said another prayer.

***

The radio barked into high-pitched life, breaking the tense silence that had formed between Edwards and Park.

"Dispatch to Detective Edwards."

Park threw a glance towards his partner, reached over and grabbed the radio receiver. "This is Park and Edwards, go ahead."

"We've got a probable hit on the plate Edwards put that BOLO on."

Detective Edwards perked up, her interest captured. She motioned with her free hand. Park passed across the radio handheld. "This is Edwards, copy that. What's the situation?"

"Patrolman reports the driver doing almost twice the speed-limit over on highway two-thirty-one," the dispatcher said, voice crackling through the radio.

Edwards sat a little straighter in the driver's seat, her eyes flicking towards her partner. For all his talk about "going where you're needed" and "ending up where you want to go," Park thought she was stretching a little too much in wanting to track down the driver of the car near the scene of the Magini's Drugs fire. Edwards may not have been the smartest detective, but she was one of the most dogged. When she got a whiff of something, she simply wasn't capable of letting it go, and something about that guy she'd seen—one Alfonse Vacarro, as she learned from the license plate's registry—stunk. She planned to look for a jacket on him as soon as she was back at the station-house, then decided to just go with her gut. At the very least, she had him on failing to obey a lawful command.

She and her partner were on their way to Vacarro's residence in the suburbs, Edwards hoping to speak with him, Park prepared to apologize for wasting his time.

Now, here Vacarro was, apparently having a second run-in with law enforcement a little over an hour later. And not just a run-in, a telling one: driving twice the speed-limit after racing off on foot, even after she'd identified herself as police.

Edwards really didn't believe in coincidences.

"Got it, thanks. Edwards out." She resisted looking smug as she handed the radio back to Park, pressing her foot to the gas-pedal. She allowed herself a tight little smile as she reached for the dash-mounted flasher.

18

"What about school? I've got a geography test on Friday."

Lexi tried to keep the exasperation from her voice. "I'll call the school from grandma's house. If we aren't back by Friday, I'm sure Mrs. Keenegan will let you take a make-up test, okay?" She zipped up Beth's overnight bag, slung the strap over her shoulder and added, "Now go help your brother finish packing his bag, please. I'll bring this downstairs. You've got five minutes, okay?"

Beth's already-knit brows drew closer together and her face scrunched up into the expression that meant she was struggling not to let her anger out. Lexi loved how important school was to Beth. How many kids got upset at the idea of missing a test? And she was proud of the girl's independence, too – of how Beth was able to think for herself, to set her own priorities. It was a rare and precious quality in a ten-year-old. But sometimes she wished her daughter would just do what she was damned well told without argument.

Her thoughts drifted back to Al's call, to the tone of his voice and the undercurrent beneath the anger. It was fear, she'd realized; the same fear she was trying to hide from the kids now as she hurried them through the rushed process of packing for a trip of indeterminate length. These last couple of years, Al's emotions swung freely between anger and apathy, at least where Lexi was concerned, interspersed with efforts at being the loving father she knew he still desperately wanted to be. But in all of their years together, fear wasn't anything she ever remembered in her husband. And that was maybe what scared her the most.

What the hell is going on? ran through her head, over and over, like the world's worst mantra.

She tamped those thoughts down, set her face into a mask of parental authority, looked Beth straight in the eye and said, "March, young lady," in as calm a voice as she could manage. "I said five minutes and the clock's ticking."

Beth opened her mouth, but snapped it shut again, deciding against whatever she was going to say. She turned on her heel and left the room, leaving Lexi alone.

Lexi took a deep breath, held it, let it out again and with its release, seemed to sag in upon herself, like a balloon with an untied tail. The weight of the bag slung across her shoulder suddenly seemed impossibly heavy and she wanted nothing more than to let it drag her down to the floor, to keep sinking, to disappear out of sight, out of range of all of the sick, sad strangeness of the world.

The sound of the doorbell ringing downstairs, slightly muted by distance, followed by Beth crying, "I'll get it!" brought Lexi back to herself. She moved from Beth's room, out into the hallway, stepping out in time to intercept the girl with an upraised hand. "No, I will. I'm going down anyway. Help your brother like I asked you to. Please."

Beth scowled and made a noise in her throat, but turned sulkily away.

Is a little obedience too much to ask? Lexi shook her head, turned towards the stairs.

Before she set foot on the first step, the doorbell rang again, followed instantly by a heavy pounding on the door.

"I'm coming! Hold on a second!" she called down the stairs, but instead of satisfying whoever was at the door, it seemed only to embolden, or perhaps annoy, them as the knocking on the door became heavier and more rapid.

Lexi moved down the stairs quickly, tossing Beth's bag aside at the landing midway down. "Get ready for an ass-chewing, whoever you are," she muttered. "This is the last thing I need today."

The pounding stopped by the time her foot hit the faded, green runner that led from the stairs towards the entryway. Unlikely as it seemed, she wondered for a moment if whoever so desperately wanted her attention a moment before had simply gone away.

And then, with a cracking like the breaking of bones, the door crashed open, splinters from the ruined frame fanning out to scatter across the entryway rug like specks of wooden snow. Lexi's heart jumped into her throat and she took a step backwards as the door swung in hard enough to bounce off of the long, narrow table next to the doorway, upsetting the shallow clay bowl that she and Al stored their car-keys in and the flowerpot that sat next to it. Drawn by the motion, Lexi's eyes went to the bowl as it teetered on the edge of the table, wobbling back and forth, threatening to drop at any moment until a form stepped between it and her, obscuring her view.

Stunned to near-numbness, she took in the sight of the pale young man who stood in the front hallway of her home: his thick, black hair, slicked back against his skull; the whiteness of his skin that was only a shade or two away from the pallor of sickness; the white sport-jacket over a black turtleneck that further accentuated his paleness; the golden crucifix hanging on a chain from his throat, catching the light for an instant as he entered the house. She guessed his age at early twenties, and with his high forehead and aquiline nose, he might have been handsome despite his pastiness, if not for his close-set eyes that reminded her of a bird of prey's. Those hard, black eyes leered at her now, burning with something that seemed to be screaming of scarcely contained violence and sending cold tendrils squirming through her chest and up her spine.

Lexi instantly took all of this in and then her gaze fell to the weapon clutched in the strange young man's hand: a huge, gleaming, long-barreled revolver like something out of a Clint Eastwood movie. The woman's eyes flicked back up towards the youth's and caught there, his strange eyes pinning her in place like a serpent staring down a mouse.

The corners of his mouth twitched upwards in a parody of a smile. "Hiya, Missus V," he said, in a voice thick with a New Jersey accent and higher-pitched than she would have guessed.

The contrast between the man's appearance and his voice was enough to break the spell he held over her. She turned without a word, scrambling back up the stairs.

Too late.

Benny closed the distance between them in a flash, his free hand snaking out to latch onto Lexi's ankle, pulling her off balance, causing her to tumble back down the stairs on her belly, the side of her head caroming off the banister as she slipped and her chin bouncing off of the thinly carpeted wooden stairs when she landed.

She rolled over onto her back, groaning, stars swimming in her vision as she opened her eyes and looked upwards into the grinning face and gaping gun-barrel of the intruder.

Lexi screamed.

19

The gray Crown Victoria eased into the driveway of the light-yellow bungalow near the end of the quiet cul-de-sac. Al put the vehicle into park and took a deep breath, trying to still the hammering in his chest. The situation was bad enough, there was no point in seeming frantic and worrying Lexi or the kids even more than they already must be. He'd made record time – he even lost that damned speed-trap cop somewhere along the way. Everything would be fine.

Al unbuckled his seatbelt, closed his eyes, inhaled deeply through his mouth and slowly let the breath out through his nose. He opened his eyes, actually felt the slightest bit better – and then he noticed the front door, open and hanging askew in the doorframe.

Stepping out of the car, teeth clenched, Al took an entirely different kind of breath and prepared himself.

Reaching into his coat, he slipped the Browning automatic from its resting place beneath his shoulder and moved up onto the porch, carefully avoiding the creaky second step. He peered through the broken door into the familiar space of the front hallway, at the mess that was made of it. The entryway table lay on the floor, one leg crooked in its mounting. The ceramic bowl and small potted plant that always stood on the table both lay in pieces on the floor amidst scattered potting soil, broken leaves, and thin, gnarled roots. The narrow green carpet that lined the hallway, leading towards the stairs, was pushed to one side and bunch up, as if something had been dragged across it.

Cautiously, eyes open for movement, ears alert for even the smallest sound, Al crossed the threshold. A dull ache began to spread through his chest with the realization that no matter how the day ended, this house would never again be a home.

A quick survey of the first floor showed nothing out of the ordinary outside from the entryway – and no occupants. Within seconds, Al returned to the front hallway, glanced around at the mess which seemed to form a clear trail towards the stairs themselves and up to the second floor. Sweat sprang from his palms. He wiped his free hand on his pants, shifted his gun to it then wiped his right hand as he peered up the stairs. From the landing, six steps up, a family portrait taken when Kyle was still in diapers stared back down at him.

"Lexi? Kids?" Al called, trying to keep a tremor from his voice.

The response came from directly overhead: a rhythmic thumping, like someone banging their heel against the thickly carpeted floor.

Al's stomach did a rapid flip-flop as he dashed up the stairs, taking them two at a time, gun leading the way. At the top he called out again: "Lexi?"

From the master bedroom, muffled by distance and the door, he heard his name. "Al?"

He was too late. Al knew that. But what choice did he have?

The bedroom door was closed as he approached. "Lexi? You in there?"

"Al… I'm sorry!" came the strained reply. "We were packing, like you told me, but—"

The sharp sound of flesh impacting flesh interrupted her, accompanied by a yelp of pain, followed instantly by a growled, "Shut the hell up."

Al growled, too, deep in his throat, a sound of bestial rage. He twisted the bedroom door's knob, threw it open with enough force that it smacked loudly against the doorstop, the way a palm had smacked Lexi's mouth a moment earlier.

Inside Al's bedroom, Benny sat on the edge of the king-sized bed, Lexi seated on his lap like a kid visiting a department store Santa Claus. The venetian blinds were drawn, but only turned halfway down, throwing bars of alternating light and shadow across the room. Benny's left forearm was pressed against Lexi's throat, restraining her, and his absurdly huge, chrome-plated pistol was held to her temple, further pinning her in place. A trickle of blood seeped from the corner of her mouth and her eyes were red and swollen; the left one was already beginning to blacken. In the far corner of the room, near the closet, Beth and Kyle huddled together, arms entangled, wrapped around each other as if each child was the other's life preserver in a storm-tossed sea. At the sight of her father, Beth's eyes went wide and wild with the hope that rescue was at hand.

Kyle choked out, "Dad!" then began to cry, huge tears racing down his cheeks. Beth threw a frantic glance towards the back of the man who held her mother, then hugged the boy closer to her chest, stroking his hair gently and making shushing noises.

Al's blood turned painfully hot in his veins, his vision grew dark, and his temples began to throb. "Lexi. Kids."

Benny smiled, his face partially obscured by the crazy tangle of Lexi's hair. "You sure got here fast, man."

Al struggled with the murderous intent that threatened to explode, to propel him across the seven feet between them and tear Benny limb from limb with his bare hands. When he spoke, his voice was flat, but the tone was deadly: "Benny, let them go."

"Why?" Benny asked, deadpan, voice as controlled as Al's. He ground the barrel of his pistol into Lexi's temple, causing her to whimper in pain. Casually, as if not even aware of what he was doing, he continued, "So you got an easier time gunnin' me down?"

There was no decision to make. Al tossed his gun away, towards the near corner of the room where Lexi's dresser and makeup table sat. He raised his hands, eyes locked with Benny's. "There. Gun's gone, I'm unarmed. Now please, Benny, let them *go*."

Benny smiled. "Why should I? Seems to me you just made this thing a whole lot easier for me."

Al bared his teeth in a silent snarl, biting back what he wanted to say. Instead: "Because it's *wrong*, Benny. Because it's *evil*. Even you should be able to see that."

Benny's face darkened, the smile disappearing into the anger that closed over his pale features like a cloud obscuring the moon. "Oh, yeah?" His voice was strangely soft. "Even me? Benny, the dumb piece of shit? The stupid fuck you got saddled with?"

Al waved his hands as if he could disperse the idea from the air. "I didn't mean it like that. *Please*, Benny."

Benny spat on the floor between them, the white gob showing in stark contrast against the dark-blue carpet. "Fuck you, you didn't. You been treatin' me like a retarded little kid since we first met. Why? Cuz you don't think I belong? Cuz Castella's my pop's cousin and *I* didn't have to work my way in like *you* did, even though your dad was Castella's buddy?" He made a scornful sound, blowing a wet puff of air through his pursed lips, like a half-assed Bronx cheer. "You ever heard of working smarter not harder, Al?"

Lexi's eyes flew around the room, from down at the arm of man who held her in a vice-grip, up to her husband, briefly making eye-contact. Al forced himself to look away, to keep his eyes on Benny, as he shook his head. "This has got nothin' to do with any that, Benny. I don't know *why* you're doin' this."

"Fuck you again, Al, you lyin' sack of shit. You know exactly what this is about. I put up with all the crap you gave me cuz you were supposed to be showin' me the ropes. I figured it was just a little – whatta ya call it? Hazing? The kid from back east gettin' his due, right? But then today you crossed a line when you treated me like a little bitch in front of that worthless old fuck, Magini. How am I supposed to ignore that, Al? Huh?"

"He's so worthless, why do you care what he thinks, Benny?" Al inched forward, hoping Benny's anger, his ranting, would distract him.

It didn't. Benny made a shooing motion with his gun. "Keep your distance." Al's head bobbed in a gesture of mea culpa as he complied, moving backwards a step.

Benny surprised him by answering his question of a moment earlier. "Cuz I *care*, okay? Cuz I'm a fuckin' *Castella* whether you like it not and I deserve *respect*. You know..." He paused. "Mister Castella, cousin Eddie, he told me once, when my pop and I visited back when I was a kid, how much he likes you. He said you got some funny ideas about, like, *honor* or some shit, but that you were still a good guy. And a few weeks ago, when I told him I wanted to work for him, he said that you were the guy to learn from, that you'd show me all the ins and outs of the business. *He* cares what you think—at least he used to—so I did, too... for a little while, anyway."

From the far corner of the bedroom, one of the children—whether Beth or Kyle, Al couldn't tell—made a sudden, high-pitched whimpering sound. Benny whirled, twisting like a contortionist to point his weapon at the kids while keeping one arm around Lexi's throat. Gun in hand, Benny didn't say a word, and the other man's expression was hidden from Al by their positions, but the sudden tang of urine filled the air as at least one of the kids' bladders released.

The scene held for a moment. No one spoke or moved. Al scarcely dared even to breathe with his children literally under the gun, only feet away and him helpless to do anything.

Back still turned, Benny broke the silence. "I hear you used'a be good, Al. A real hard-case. Castella said so himself. And I heard it from other guys, too, when I asked around about you."

Al shifted his stance, sliding to his right enough so that he could see Benny's profile, see his eyes locked on Beth and Kyle, who stared back, raptly frozen, like newborn rabbits under the gaze of a swooping owl or a pair of deer caught in an oncoming truck's headlights. Al squeezed his own eyes shut, squeezing back the hot, angry, frustrated tears that threatened to spill forth.

"But then you got soft," Benny continued, his voice deceptively gentle now. "Cuz of these two."

Benny turned from the kids, apparently satisfied that there would be no more interruptions from the pair or maybe just no longer caring. Benny's attention returned to Al, his gun-hand swinging back around in a wide, lazy arc as if the huge pistol weighed no more than his empty hand. His eyes met Al's; the placidity they held was somehow more frightening than the fury. Al shivered.

"And cuz of *this* bitch!" Benny suddenly roared, shoving the barrel of the gun deep into Lexi's cheek, hard enough to tear the skin and bring a shriek to her lips. Benny's left arm uncoiled from around Lexi's throat, moving behind her head, his fingers tangling in her hair and jerking her head back, exposing the softness of her throat. Directly into her ear, spittle flying from his lips, Benny screamed, "This bitch *right here*! Trapped ya, huh, Al? How'd it go? She tell ya' the condom broke and she's got one in the oven? She say you had to 'do the right thing' and marry her?"

"Stop!" Al cried.

Benny ignored him, twisted Lexi's head around and pushed her face forwards and up, only an inch or two from his own. "So I figure," he leered directly into her eyes, teeth bared, breath coming fast and hard as if he was approaching some sort of climax, "if they're the problem, I got the solution."

He broke off his glare, turning towards Al again. "I figured I'd just get rid 'em for you. Get you back on track. Give you another shot at glory, you know?"

Al's mind raced. He'd been wrong. Benny wasn't simply wild – he was flat-out insane.

What the fuck do I do? he screamed inside his own head. *What the fuck do I do?*

"But then I realized," Benny continued, "you probably wouldn't be real pleased, if I did. I mean, whatever the reason, you seem pretty damned attached to these fuckers. That whore at the club, maybe you'd let that go, but not these three."

Lexi's eyes, red and crazed, ping-ponged back and forth between Benny and Al, asking questions, the answers to which didn't matter. Al tried not to meet her eyes – not out of guilt, but rather a need to keep from any distractions as his mind frantically worked, trying to hit on some solution, some conclusion that didn't end in blood.

He couldn't think of one, but he had to do *something*.

"Benny," Al began.

The other man ignored him, intent on continuing his speech. Al wondered momentarily, absurdly, if Benny had practiced it. He imagined the kid reciting it out loud to himself, practicing his expressions in the rearview mirror on the drive out to the suburbs.

"You wouldn't let that go, Al. I just know you wouldn't. And if I did that, you wouldn't want to keep working for Mister," *Mis-tuh*, "Castella. But you know what, Al? I do. I like it a real whole lot. And this crap between you and me is really gettin' in the way. It's just gotta end." Benny sighed heavily, as if the weight of the world rested on his bony shoulders. The barrel of his gun swung up towards Al. "So I guess I'll just get rid of you, instead."

Al was out of chances, but Lexi saw hers. She grabbed Benny's gun-arm with both hands, yanked it close and sank her teeth into his exposed wrist, hard enough that something inside made a cracking sound.

"Fuck!" Benny shrieked, drawing the word out into a howl of pain as his uninjured arm flailed, shoving the woman away, dumping her to the floor as he jumped to his feet. "You crazy bitch!"

Lexi scrambled away from Benny on all fours. Al, with a roar of desperate fury, dove in, crossing the space between them in a flash of movement, tackling the smaller man around the waist, knocking them both to the floor.

"Get offa me!" Benny shouted, throwing his injured arm up over his face, blocking Al's swinging fist.

"Lexi!" Al barked. "Get outta here! Get the kids and *go!*"

The two men scrabbled in the narrow space between the bed and the wall. Benny, injured, frenzied with pain and fury, fought like a cornered rat, but Al was heavier and fighting for something more than just himself.

"Get the fuck off me!" Benny shrieked. "Cousin Eddie'll kill you for this!"

Al dealt an openhanded slap to the other man, bouncing Benny's head against the floor, hard, dazing him and shutting his mouth for the moment. Al straddled the younger man's chest, pinning Benny's arms against the carpet with his knees.

"You crazy piece'a shit!" Al screamed, swinging first one fist then the other downwards, slamming into Benny's face again and again, alternating left and right with a sickening rhythm, pounding a savage beat on the pinned man's flesh.

Thump! Thump! Thump!

"Burn an old man outta his home!"

Thump! Thump! Thump!

"Beat Jenna half to death!"

Thump! Thump! Thump!

"Threaten my family…"

Thump! Thump! Thump!

His breath was coming hard and ragged, his overworked lungs refusing to fill, but he couldn't stop. He had to get the words out. "Then try to kill me – all because I don't live up to *your* expectations?"

Over and over, Al's fists fell, mashing Benny's features beyond any hope of recognition. Benny was long unconscious, but Al wasn't done.

"You're worthless, Benny!" He had lost all feeling in his hands; part of him suspected they were both shattered, as damaged as the bloodied pulp he'd made of the young Castella's face.

"Doesn't matter what your fuckin' name is or who you're related to, you're nothin' but a worthless, psychotic piece of trash!"

For long moments, Al continued – until his breath would scarcely come and he could barely lift his arms, until the blows to Benny were little more than symbols of Al's vengeance, of his anger, of his shame that he'd let things get this bad. Then he climbed off of the quivering, bleeding mess he'd made, heedless of the damage to his own body or the blood he was splattered in, and struggled to his feet.

"Why…" Forming words was an effort and even then they came out in a choked sob. "Why Castella even gave you a chance, what he saw in you… why I didn't say something to him sooner, before we got here, I'll never… know."

Al stooped, retrieved Benny's gun from where it had fallen. He stood straight again, needing both ruined hands to clasp the huge pistol, pointing it towards the center of the wreck that had been a young man's face. "And frankly, I don't really give a shit anymore."

"Police! Drop the weapon!"

The shout came suddenly and was so unexpected that for a moment, the words didn't make sense. Al turned slowly, looking back over his shoulder to see a middle-aged, red-headed woman in a hip-length coat training a gun on him. Behind her, a bald Asian man and a trio of uniformed police officers likewise had weapons aimed in his direction.

What the fuck are they doin' in my house? was his first, ridiculous thought. And as the adrenaline began to fade, as details began to take shape through the white-hot, blood-red haze in his mind, it all seemed suddenly quite natural.

"No! Stop!" Lexi appeared between Al and the cops, arms spread wide, as if to shield him from their attention and the consequences of what he'd done. "My husband was protecting us!" she cried. "This man broke in, kicked the door down and —"

"It's okay, baby," Al cut in, tossing Benny's gun towards the lady cop's feet. "I got this."

Images flashed through Al's brain:

Eddie Castella, alcohol-flushed and unguarded for once in his life, looking him in the eye and saying, *"Don't let this be your life."*

Mike, sad and sympathetic, as he told his cousin, *"You gotta find your own way out."*

Lexi, wild-eyed and terrified, with a madman's arm wrapped around her throat.

155

Beth looking to him with hope written across her every feature, as she shielded her little brother's body with her own.

Kyle, crying out, "*Dad!*" at the sight of Al's sudden appearance in the darkest moment of his young life.

Benny Castella, bleeding, ruined, but still breathing, at that very moment lying on the floor of the bedroom Al had slept in for fourteen years.

Al locked eyes with Nicole Edwards, slowly raised his hands above his head and, in a voice that seemed distant and oddly formal, said, "My name is Al Vacarro. I've been a member of the Castella organization since I was sixteen years old, and I'll tell you anything you want to know if you can promise to keep my family safe."

End

ABOUT THE AUTHOR

Brandon Barrows is the award-nominated author of the occult-noir novel *This Rough Old World* as well as over fifty published stories, selected of which have been collected into the books *The Altar in the Hills* and *The Castle-Town Tragedy*. He is also the writer of nearly one-hundred individual comic book issues. He is an active member of the Private Eye Writers of America.

NOTE FROM THE AUTHOR

Word-of-mouth is crucial for any author to succeed. If you enjoyed *Burn Me Out*, please leave a review online—anywhere you are able. Even if it's just a sentence or two. It would make all the difference and would be very much appreciated.

Thanks!
Brandon